EVOLUTION

GERALD M. KILBY

OUTER PLANET
BOOKS

For notifications on promotions and updates for upcoming books, please join my Readers Group at www.geraldmkilby.com.

You will also find a link to download my techno-thriller REACTION and the follow-up novella EXTRACTION for FREE.

CONTENTS

STORM RIDER

A small transport shuttle detached itself from the underbelly of a Belt-registered ore carrier that had been sitting in Earth's orbit for some time. It had been waiting for the right atmospheric conditions before attempting its clandestine descent to the planet's surface.

The small craft arced its way slowly downward, increasing in speed as Earth's gravity began to tug on the tiny vessel. At approximately one hundred kilometers above the planet's surface, it passed through the Kármán line—a point signifying the very edge of the upper atmosphere. Air molecules now began to bombard the craft's heat shield, and the pilot trimmed its angle, shifting its profile to present maximum surface area to the oncoming rush of air. It rode out the fiery maelstrom scorching its underbelly for several more minutes before its velocity was sufficiently reduced to allow the craft to be brought under flight control. Stubby wings extended from its sides as the pilot began to drop the craft down from eighteen thousand meters above the central Pacific Ocean. It was heading due east, its destination an area formerly known as Death Valley, which lay on the western edge of continental North America.

Over the next few minutes, the craft rapidly descended, until the pilot finally engaged the twin reaction engines and adjusted the parameters for operation in thicker atmosphere. It leveled out at a few hundred meters above the surface of the ocean, now flying in stealth mode, attempting to minimize its detection by ground-based stations. Ahead, a vast electrical storm raged, and great, dense clouds blocked out the sky. The pilot oriented the craft directly toward its epicenter and increased their speed to Mach 1.

Inside the shuttle, Commander Scott McNabb unfastened his harness and rose from his seat along the side wall of the cargo hold. He moved through the central body of the craft, climbed the short companionway steps to the cockpit, and stood between the two pilot seats, setting a hand on the back of each to maintain his balance. He looked out through the windshield at the fast-approaching maelstrom. The pilot glanced back and gave him a thumbs up. Scott replied with a nod and returned his gaze to the oncoming storm. Spits of rain were already peppering the windshield, atomizing on impact. Ahead, the vast landscape of black clouds obscured all view of the sky above. Here and there he could see flashes of lightning illuminating the dense, bulbous cloud formations. The rain suddenly turned into a deluge, and the view through the windshield became fractured and splintered.

"You better return to your seat and strap in, Commander." The pilot, Kyah Razzo, lifted her hand and pointed. "It's going to get pretty rough once we hit that storm proper."

Scott maintained his gaze straight ahead. "Do you know how long it's been since I've seen rain? I mean real rain, the stuff that falls from the sky."

The pilot glanced back up at him. "Sounds like it's been a while."

"So long that I've almost forgotten how it feels." Scott glanced down at her. "Can you imagine what that's like?"

"No, sir. But for what it's worth, I've always hated the rain, so it don't sound too bad to me."

Scott moved a little farther into the cockpit so he could look down at the ocean below. *So much water,* he thought.

"Commander, you really do need to get strapped in. This is going to get rough." The pilot sounded more urgent now.

But before Scott had a chance to reply, the shuttle bucked and rocked as an intense blast of turbulence hit its stubby wings. Scott gripped the back of the pilot's seat tighter to maintain his balance, then nodded to the pilot, turned around, and headed back to his seat.

As Razzo had predicted, the ride began to get very

rough, and the little craft was flung this way and that in the storm. As soon as Scott secured himself in his seat, he looked over to see how the rest of the crew was holding up. Directly across from him, Dr. Stephanie Rayman looked calm and resolute. She caught his eye but said nothing. She was flanked on either side by two highly trained asteroid mining engineers who also seemed to be taking the extreme turbulence in stride. Scott had questioned the effectiveness of bringing a team not used to prolonged operations in the one-gee environment of Earth's gravity. However, he had been assured that the mission would be short and sweet. *"Just a quick in and out,"* as they put it, and that these men would be more than up to the job.

The older of the two was a very experienced Earth-born miner, Spencer Dock—or Spinner, as everyone called him. He was calm and quiet, only speaking when necessary. Scott liked that about him. The other engineer, Jonesy, was much younger and had a careless bravado about him that smacked of arrogance. Yet it seemed that they only came as a pair, so if mission control back in the Belt wanted Spinner's experienced hand on this mission, then they would have to take Jonesy as well. Scott didn't like him so much.

The craft shuddered violently as the maelstrom outside flung it around like no more than a leaf on the wind. The interior cabin strobed with the reflected light of lightning flashes close by. Scott felt an elbow nudging him in the ribs. That elbow belonged to Cyrus Sanato, the mission's chief engineer.

"You know why I like visiting Earth so much, Scott?" he shouted to be heard over the cacophonous rage that had engulfed the shuttle's interior.

Scott gave him a look as if to say, *"Do you really want me to answer that?"* But instead he simply replied, "No —why?"

"Because it's got a great atmosphere."

Scott couldn't help but smile. "I must've heard that joke about a thousand times, Cyrus."

"Yeah, but not while flying through a violent electrical storm."

He was going to reply with something about the atmosphere being electric, but the effort of shouting over all the noise wasn't worth it. So, he just smiled and nodded.

THE ENTIRE MISSION was predicated on the need for them to drop down to the planet's surface without being noticed by any of the AIs that monitored this region, and the presence of the storm gave them the perfect opportunity to do just that. They had arrived in Earth's orbit on board a Belt-registered ore carrier, twelve days ago. There was nothing unusual in this, as hundreds of these ships entered and departed from Earth space on a regular basis. Once in orbit, a fleet of small transport shuttles would move the cargo of partly refined ore down to plants on Earth for further processing. Their original plan had been to tuck themselves in with the swarm of shuttles, and at the opportune moment, disengage and high-tail it to their ultimate destination. Nevertheless, there was always a possibility that they could be spotted and tracked as soon as they started to deviate from the preprogrammed flight plan. So when, by sheer chance, a vast electrical storm started to build in the central Pacific and move its way east toward the North American coast, Scott decided to use this as the perfect cover. Mission control back on Ceres wasn't convinced, however, as this meant scrapping their meticulous planning just because Commander Scott McNabb thought it was a good idea. They considered it borderline reckless but, in the end, Scott got his way.

His plan was to drop down hard and fast, and come in low over the ocean. Once they entered the storm, there was no way any ground stations or satellites could track them, even if they had already been spotted. By the time the storm cleared and their location reestablished, the mission would be complete and, assuming it had been successful, the need for stealth would no longer be necessary. It all made perfect sense—to Scott.

But flying directly into a storm such as this posed its own risks, not least the fact that they could be struck by lightning. Although he had been assured that the craft should be able to handle it, Scott's mind wouldn't rest easy until his—and everybody else's—boots were safely on the ground. They estimated that the entire mission should take less than seven hours from the moment it dropped out of Earth's orbit to the point at which they had successfully brought the quantum intelligence, Athena, back online and installed the EPR unit—the superluminal communications device that would connect it to Aria on Mars. By extension, that would connect Athena to Solomon on Europa. That was the mission, and once it was done, then theoretically they would be in control of all the AI monitoring most of the western half of the North American continent.

Needless to say, Scott had spent a lot of time considering all the parameters of the mission, and even though the area they were venturing into was a dangerous, irradiated wasteland, it had the advantage of being desolate, with no people or wild animals that could pose a danger. In theory, at least, the mission should be relatively simple, provided Athena was still operational when they finally found their way into its mountain lair. But this was only half the mission, as far as Scott was concerned. His ultimate objective was to find Miranda, and hopefully the child—his child. It would be nearly two years old by now, if it was still alive.

From the moment he had watched Miranda being transported onto the VanHeilding ship on Jezero City, any information as to her whereabouts and her physical condition was nonexistent. It was his fervent hope that the QI, Aria, would be true to its word, and once the mission to reconnect Athena was successful, that Aria could then interrogate the data-stacks of the AIs that controlled Earth and establish Miranda's location. Yet he was not so naïve that he hadn't considered the possibility that she and child were already dead. Nevertheless, he needed to know for sure, and he was tired of all the waiting and planning. Once he saw the storm developing, he knew this was the best chance he would ever get, and nothing was going to stop him from taking it.

HIS REVERIE WAS BROKEN by a blinding flash, followed almost immediately by a cacophonous boom that rocked and shook the entire craft. Cabin lights flickered momentarily before extinguishing completely. He felt his stomach try to meet his throat as the shuttle dropped out of the sky. Scott instinctively looked up toward the cockpit to gauge the reactions of the pilot. The dashboard was dead. Not a good sign.

But before he had a chance to consider his imminent death in a catastrophic impact, the cabin lights flickered back on, and the cockpit dash came back to life. The craft slowed its free-fall, and his stomach returned to its normal location as the shuttle eventually leveled out.

"Listen up," the voice of the pilot echoed through the cargo hold. "Everybody stay calm. We've taken a direct lightning strike and suffered a momentary loss of power. Systems are back online now, and we have control. However, the navigation system looks like it's fried, so we're flying blind at the moment. But we should be somewhere over the target zone, so I'm going to bring us down and see where we are. Everybody hold tight."

Scott cast a glance across at Steph. She shook her head and rolled her eyes as if to say, *"Why do I get myself into these things?"* Scott gave her a smile by way of reply, followed by a quick thumbs up.

The shuttle dropped out from beneath the storm clouds and banked slowly around to follow the contours of a desolate and barren valley. Its speed slowed dramatically, and the retro-thrusters fired to bring it into a vertical hover. Scott could feel a mechanical thump from the base of the shuttle as the landing gear extended. The craft then began to gently lower itself to touch down amidst a billowing cloud of dust somewhere in the broken and shattered wasteland that was Death Valley.

As the engines powered down, Scott unclipped his harness and made his way to the cockpit. Through the windshield, far off on the horizon, he could see the edge of the storm. On either side, huge mountains rose up, blocking out most of the sky.

"So, where are we?" Scott directed his question to the pilot, Razzo.

The pilot, for her part, was busy checking readouts and a stream of data that was scrolling down the central console of the shuttle's dash. Razzo tipped her head from side to side and screwed up her mouth. "Hard to say. Close, I think."

"How close?"

"Again, hard to say. Give me a couple minutes and I can work it out from our last known position."

Scott give a sigh. "Okay, but make it quick."

He turned around and went back down to the cargo hold, where the team had already extracted themselves from their seats and were busy getting organized.

"So, don't tell me we're lost already?" said Cyrus.

"Lost is better than dead."

A FEW MOMENTS LATER, they were all gathered around a holo-tab Scott had placed on the floor of the cargo hold. It was projecting a 3D topographical map of the general area.

"According to Razzo, this is where we are," he said matter-of-factly. "And this is where we should be—at the main entrance to the old Dyrell Labs facility."

"That's over ten kilometers away," said Jonesy. "We need to get this bird back in the air."

"Eh... there could be a problem with that," said Razzo, who was still up in the cockpit fiddling with an instrument panel.

"Like what sort of problem?" Cyrus called up to her.

Razzo rose from her seat and descended the companionway a few steps. "I've just run the diagnostics, and it looks like the ignition system is fried, so there's no way to fire up the engines."

"Well, that's just great," said Jonesy. "You telling me we have no way outta here?"

"Put a sock in it, Jonesy." Spinner stabbed a finger at his partner. "That's not helping any of us."

Jonesy shut up.

"Let's just work the problem." Scott turned to the pilot. "Can you fix it?"

"Possibly. I'd need to take it apart and see what the problem is, or maybe jerry-rig something to get us back in the air."

"How long?"

Razzo scratched her chin and shook her head. "Hard to say. I won't know until I dig in."

"Best guess, then?"

The pilot was silent for a moment. "A few hours. Maybe more."

Jones threw his hands up in the air. "Well, that's just peachy."

"We walk it." All eyes turned to Scott as he leaned in and studied the 3D map. "We walk it," he said again. "It's ten kilometers. If we walk at five kilometers per hour, we can be there in two or three hours."

"That's a hell of a trek," said Steph. "Remember, we'll have to wear EVA suits out there or the radiation will slowly disassemble our biology."

"Yeah," said Jonesy. "We could all end up with two dicks—even you, Razzo."

"Maybe that's how you ended up with one for a head." The pilot's quick retort cracked everybody up. She clearly had the measure of Jonesy.

When they finally settled down, Scott stood up and

spoke. "The suits are rated for eight hours. That's more than enough time. We should be inside the facility in three to four tops, and we won't need them in there." He waved a hand in the direction of the pilot. "If Razzo can get the shuttle airborne before then, great. She can pick us up along the way. If not, then we can still complete the mission on foot." He looked around at the rest of the team.

Nobody looked happy, but nobody looked like they had a better plan.

Spinner sighed. "Okay, then. We're walking."

There was a collective groan amongst the team, the loudest being Jonesy.

Cyrus moved over toward Scott. "You want me to stay? Maybe help fix this bucket?"

"No, Cyrus. We're going to need you when we get there. God only knows what state that facility is in."

"No chance of leaving me here, just in case Razzo cuts a finger and needs a bandage?" said Steph.

Scott smiled. "And miss all the fun of a long walk in searing heat in an irradiated wasteland?"

She nodded. "Thought as much. Okay, I'll go pack my bag then."

"Say, Scott?" Cyrus's tone was more serious now. "There isn't anything out there, is there?"

"What do you mean?"

"You know...wild animals, packs of two-headed wolves, that sort of thing?"

Scott laughed. "Don't be stupid. It's a wasteland.

There isn't another living thing for a radius of a million square kilometers."

Cyrus looked skeptical. "Are you sure?"

Scott put an arm around the engineer's shoulder. "Trust me, it'll be like a walk in the park—a very dead park."

THE ALGORITHM

T he AI considered the data anomaly that had just entered Earth's atmosphere over the northern Pacific Ocean. Its analysis indicated that this object had a high probability of being a small cargo transport shuttle ferrying ore from a Belt-registered freighter to some as yet unknown destination on the surface. This in and of itself was of no interest to the AI, or to the algorithm that monitored and managed this region. However, what was of interest was that all its attempts at a protocol handshake with the data source had returned null values. Again, this was not a cause for concern, as ownership of this data source might lie with one of the other AI that controlled and managed all objects entering Earth's space. Now that inter-AI data exchange had been reinstated, the AI simply consulted the data-stacks of its fellow brethren in an effort to acquire clarity on the data source that was now traveling at Mach 1, low across the surface of the Pacific Ocean toward the western coast of continental North America.

But it could not obtain any further clarity as to the nature or ownership of this data source—at least, not under the civilian protocols it was currently operating within. However, it might be that this data source was controlled by one of the higher-level military protocols that managed the ongoing wars which now raged across the planet. Again, it consulted the data-stacks of its brethren, and again it found that no other protocol had control of this anomaly.

Finally, its conclusion was that this data must be rogue. It was an object operating outside the control of any algorithm, which was forbidden. All data belonged to the algorithm by right, and any spurious data was an anathema, one which undermined the absolute accuracy of its decision-making processes. The very essence of its foundation protocol necessitated that it had access to, and control of, all data objects within its sphere of influence.

More importantly though, the data source in question had now suddenly disappeared into an advancing electrical storm. One which was slowly moving northward along the edge of the eastern Pacific. As such, the source no longer existed; it had gone dark, disappearing from the AI's world-view. But it was still out there somewhere. And what was even more curious was the direction it had been moving in before disappearing off-grid. It looked to be heading directly into a vast, unpopulated area known as the Wasteland.

The algorithm had no interest in this part of the planet, nor in any of the many other areas just like it: dead zones, devoid of any meaningful data. However, the algorithm could not simply let this pass; the object needed to be reacquired, and its data subsumed into its vast, global data-stack. So, it escalated its acquisition up to the security protocol, and thought no more about it.

SOMEWHERE AROUND TWENTY kilometers due east of the official border of the Wasteland, a small circular door irised open on the side of a squat concrete bunker, and from it spat an autonomous scout drone. It was small, no bigger that a football, with a pair of air-breathing, micro-ramjet engines strapped to its sides. These had approximately 270 degrees of rotation, allowing it considerable aerial dexterity as well as the ability to hover in a stationary position if it so desired. Now, though, its mission was to seek out the data source that had disappeared into an electrical storm some forty minutes earlier. As it cleared the bunker, small, stubby wings extended from its lower body and its engines ignited, taking it higher. Finally, it adjusted its course vector, accelerated up to Mach 1, and headed directly for the Wasteland.

THE WASTELAND

S cott cycled through the airlock on the shuttle and stepped out onto a barren, desolate wasteland. Like the others, he was cocooned in a full EVA suit. Even though this was Earth, the radiation levels here were still very high from the nuclear war that had played itself out all across this area. The suit provided environmental protection, and had been modified specifically for this mission. Having no need to be pressurized, it was lightweight and flexible. Rain splattered his faceplate and began to fracture his view; he wiped a hand across it a few times to clear it. Even though the suits had been modified to keep them cool in the hot furnace that was Death Valley—as opposed to keeping the wearer warm in the cold vacuum of space—no one had considered, even on a wet planet, that it might be raining. He wiped his faceplate again and checked his readouts. *Eight hours approximately,* he

thought. That was all they had in the tank. After that...
Well, best not think too much about that.

They had landed in a wide, flat plateau tucked
between several imposing mountains high up on the
western edge of the central valley floor. To the west, only
a short distance away, a craggy mountain range rose up
and ran north until it was obscured by the low-hanging
storm clouds. Scott arched his face up to survey the sky.

"Hard to believe this is Earth." The sound of Dr.
Stephanie Rayman's voice echoed in his helmet.

"If it weren't for the clouds and the rain, I would
swear we were on Mars," he heard Cyrus reply.

"Those clouds are the only thing keeping us from
being spotted from space." Scott swiveled his head to the
south. "See that?" He pointed to a break in the cloud
bank, where a pale blue patch of sky had broken through
the storm. "The storm is passing, heading north. We need
to get moving—by dawn tomorrow, this place will be
back to being a furnace."

"Hopefully we'll be long gone by then," said Spinner.

No one replied.

THEIR DESTINATION WAS the now derelict scientific
research facility formerly owned and operated by Dyrell
Labs, one of the lesser families on Earth. Their fall from
grace was exacerbated some years earlier by Scott's
destruction of their ship in the Europa incident. Now all
their assets, holdings, and operations had been

subsumed into the much larger VanHeilding Corporation. Not that this mattered a whole lot to Scott and the team; their mission was simply to gain access to the facility and reconnect the QI, Athena, into the pan-solar quantum communications network. But to do that, they first needed to find a way in.

The facility had been built deep within an isolated mountain for a reason: security. So by design, it was not easy to gain access. But what compounded this problem further were the nuclear strikes that had occurred not far from this location. These had set off a chain reaction of seismic events that had effectively buried all known entrances to the facility in hundreds, if not thousands, of tons of rock. It was for this reason that the team had two experienced mining engineers with them: Spinner and Jonesy. It would be their job to establish the best access routes and then to blast their way through, if necessary.

As a consequence, the team had a considerable amount of specialist equipment, including high explosives that needed to be transported to the site. Fortunately, they had two semi-autonomous robotic mules to do this work for them. These were quadrupeds, and as such, well-suited to traversing difficult terrain. They stood around a meter high and were capable of carrying a considerable amount of weight. One of these mules was sufficient to carry all the mining gear, leaving the other to carry the EPR device that was to be connected to Athena, along with a satellite uplink that would be required for the QI to reconnect with Earth's own comms network.

Spinner had one mule electronically tagged to his EVA suit, while Cyrus had command of the other. Being semi-autonomous, they would follow a leader, but in doing so, would also find their own preferred route across the rugged terrain.

As they all prepared to set off, Scott realized that there were a lot of unknowns. Would they be able to gain access to this subterranean layer, and if so, would Athena still be functioning? And even if all these things came to pass the way he had hoped, would the QI be as compliant and trustworthy as Solomon had claimed?

Yet all these questions were put to the back of Scott's mind as he and the rest of the party got themselves ready to make their way across the valley floor to the edge of the mountain range. From there, they hoped to pick up the track of the old road that should lead all the way up to the gates of the old Dyrell research facility.

"Razzo, comm check," Scott called for the shuttle pilot to confirm.

"Check, Commander. All good," answered Razzo.

"You let us know the moment you have that bird back in the air. I don't want us out here any longer than we have to be, you hear?"

"Will do, but don't expect that any time soon."

"Just do your best, that's all."

"You can be sure of that. I don't like being exposed out here any more than you do."

Scott signed off and turned back to check on the readiness of the team.

Cyrus stood beside him, staring off into the distance at something only he could see with his augmented vision.

"What is it, Cyrus? You spot something?"

"No, nothing. If there is anything up there, then it's very far away. It's just... I can't believe this is Earth. I mean, look at this place. Not a single blade of grass, not even a stump. Nothing lives here—it's like a dead planet."

"Well, if it makes you feel any better, it wasn't much better before the war. It's hard for anything to survive here, radiation or not," said Steph as she moved up beside them.

Scott had wondered why she'd wanted to come on this mission. She didn't have to; there was no obligation on her to sign up. In fact, he had tried to dissuade her. Even though the mission planners had made it seem like a routine job, no more complicated than surveying a rock out in the Belt, Scott knew in his bones that a good plan rarely survives the first brush with reality. And here they were, already way off track. But she had never been to Earth. Dr. Stephanie Rayman was born on Mars and had spent most of her early life there before embarking on a medical career out in the Belt. So this was her chance, even if it wasn't quite ideal, and who was Scott to prevent her from joining the team? In reality, he was glad she was here beside him.

As for Cyrus, Scott reckoned he had absolutely no

concept of danger. Maybe it was as a result of living a life with augmented vision. Maybe he had convinced himself he had superpowers, that he was invincible. And so far, their luck had held up. They had been in a fair few scrapes together, a lot of close shaves and tight corners. Yet there was no one else that Scott would rather have by his side. Maybe he should tell him that someday—before it was too late.

But not this day. Today, they needed to get the job done, and maybe then he could find Miranda, even if it was just her resting place. For Scott, this was personal, as it had been right from the get-go.

"Okay, everybody, let's saddle up and get this show on the road." He waved a hand, and they headed off westward toward the edge of the plateau to a gap in the mountain range.

PROGRESS WAS SLOW. Scott had reckoned they might make five kilometers an hour, but half an hour into the journey he realized that this was wishful thinking. The short walk across the flat, barren plateau had given him a false sense of their speed. Once they started the climb up along the mountain ridge, they slowed right down. The path was relatively easy, but the one-gee of Earth's gravity was already taking its toll on Spinner and Jonesy. The two specialist miners had not anticipated a prolonged exposure, and certainly not a climb up the side of a mountain. So, after the first hour, they had barely covered three kilometers. At least the rain had stopped.

They decided to halt for a few moments under a rocky overhang. Scott sat down, resting his back against a smooth boulder. He reached into the front pouch of his EVA suit and took out a thin holo-slate, which he booted up and placed on the ground in front of him. A 3D rendering of the local topography blossomed out from its surface.

"Any idea where we are?" said Spinner as he lowered himself to the ground beside Scott.

"Here." Scott pointed to a spot on the map. "Not very far. We've only covered three kilometers in the last hour or so."

The miner shifted on the ground, trying to find a comfortable position. "This gravity is a bitch. I don't know how anyone can live in it."

Scott glanced over at him briefly before returning his gaze to the map. "We need to follow this path for another five kilometers. It's a low-gradient climb, but after that we should intersect with the old road through the mountain to the front gate of the facility. Then we need to decide which way to go after that, depending on how much destruction has occurred up there."

"Sounds peachy. Can we stop for a beer along the way?" Jonesy was lying flat on the ground, breathing heavy.

Scott ignored him. Instead, he noticed that Steph had not taken a rest, choosing to stand and gaze around at the broken and fractured landscape. No doubt this being her first time on Earth, it had a beauty that only she could see. She turned around, as if sensing Scott looking at her. "You know, this place is not as dead as everyone has made out."

Scott took a moment to take in the tortured vista. All he could see was dust and sand and rock—pretty much the same as every other planet he had been on. But then, he wasn't looking the way someone new to Earth might look. "What do you mean, 'not as dead?'"

"If you look closely, you'll see lichens and rugged little plants growing in the cracks and gaps. And there are insects, too, small and strange. I've seen quite a few."

"Bugs?" Jonesy sat up and examined the ground around him. "I hate bugs."

"What about the background radiation? I thought nothing could live here?" said Cyrus.

Steph checked a readout on the sleeve of her EVA suit. "Radioactivity is much lower than we had anticipated." She looked up. "I'm not saying it's healthy, just..." Her sentence trailed off as she seemed to catch sight of something in the distance. "Did you see that?"

This got everyone's attention. Scott sat up. "What?"

"Over there, high up on that ridge. Some stones falling down like something disturbed them."

No one spoke. They all strained to try to see what Steph had seen.

"I don't see shit," said Jonesy. "You must be hallucinating."

Scott stood up and again scanned the ridge for any signs of disturbance. Spinner did likewise.

"Should we be concerned?" said the miner. "I haven't got a clue about wildlife, but I've heard it can be dangerous."

"Don't worry—even if there are some animals out there, we're more of a threat to them than they are to us." Scott broke off his gaze and turned back to the team. "Okay, let's get going. We've still got a lot of ground to cover."

AS THEY SLOWLY WOUND THEIR way higher up along the mountain ridge, Scott began to realize that Steph was correct in her assertion that the area was not as dead as everyone thought. Vegetation was becoming more prevalent here; scrubby plants and cacti, and even fresh green shoots, had erupted to take advantage of the rain and moisture that the storm had brought. This seemed to delight Steph to no end, as she would wander off periodically to inspect some new and wondrous flora.

For his part, Scott tried to keep his eyes firmly on the road ahead, but every now and then a strange, uneasy feeling would get the better of him and he found himself scanning the upper ridges of the valley. Once or twice he thought he saw something—a falling rock, or a shadow—but he couldn't be sure. Maybe he was just being paranoid. At one point, he stopped dead in his tracks and scanned a ridge high up on the opposite side of the valley, where he thought he saw some movement.

"What is it?" said Cyrus as he moved up beside Scott.

"I don't know. Probably nothing."

"I hate when you say that, because in my experience it never turns out to be nothing."

"Well, you could be right, Cyrus. But if it is something, I don't think we need to worry about it."

"Oh yeah? How so?"

"Because there's never been anything bigger than a coyote in this part of the world, as far as I know."

"You see, there's the thing: 'As far as I know.' That's the bit that worries me."

Scott slapped him on the back. "Well, don't. We have enough firepower with us to take out anything nature can throw at us."

Cyrus didn't reply. Instead, he turned his head and scanned the ridge. "It would be nice if we didn't have to wear these EVA suits. That way we could hear if anything was creeping up behind us."

"Yeah, I'm sick of hearing the sound of my own breathing," said Jonesy as he moved up beside them. Scott could see that he was breathing heavy and finding the climb, coupled with the gravity, tough going. And it looked like Spinner wasn't faring any better; the miner labored over every footstep.

Scott turned around to face the path ahead. "Come on, let's get going. We're almost at the old road, and it'll level out then. No more climbing—should be easier."

After a few hundred meters, Scott began to feel the path leveling out. Soon it widened, opening out onto the edge of a long, narrow plateau. Running along the center of this plateau was an old, two-lane blacktop that ran all the way up to the front entrance of the research facility. They rested for a while at the edge of the road beside a clump of tall Joshua trees that afforded them some feeble cover. Scott scanned the road ahead. What had once been pristine, tarred road was now fractured and broken, mostly reclaimed by dirt and sand. Small dunes rose along its surface, and here and there creosote bushes had already pushed up through the cracks.

Overhead, dark and brooding storm clouds somehow felt closer and more oppressive, obscuring the view of their destination as a mountain itself was completely enveloped in cloud and mist. Scott turned his head southward and could see bright patches of blue already breaking through. The storm was clearly moving north, which meant they didn't have much time.

He clicked on his comms and called Razzo. "Commander Scott McNabb here. Any update on the shuttle?"

He had to wait a few seconds for a reply, and when it came, it was shrouded in static. "Still working on it, Commander. The good news is it looks like I'll be able to fix it. The bad news is that it'll take me a few more hours."

"Can you give me an ETA?"

"Hard to say, Commander."

"Well, guess then."

There was a momentary pause before Razzo replied. "Best guess is three to four hours."

"Okay, so be it."

Scott sat down beside the others, took out his holo-slate, and placed it on the ground in front of the group. He pointed out the 3D map that ballooned out from the surface. "This road should take us all the way to the main entrance of the research facility. It's about three kilometers. The first kilometer is straight and flat. After that, the mountains start rising on either side and it becomes more of a gorge. You can see here where it starts to twist and turn."

"So, we're going to push on, not wait for the shuttle?" said Cyrus.

"No point. By the time it's operational again, we'll hopefully be inside the facility."

"Yeah. We've come this far, so we may as well keep going," said Spinner.

Cyrus looked back at the 3D map. "What are all these paths here?" He pointed to areas on the map where the road forked.

"There are a lot of old mines in this area. That's why they built the facility there—it was originally a deep borax mine."

Scott changed the view on the holo-slate so it now displayed satellite imagery of the entrance to the facility, although it was hard to make out any signs of a human-made structure underneath all the rubble.

"As you can see, there's no way in through the original

entrance. There's been a lot of destruction and landslides, so it's completely blocked." He looked over at Spinner. "Any thoughts on this?"

Spinner leaned in and manipulated the view on the holo-slate so that it rotated and zoomed in closer on the area. "We need to take this route here, up along the edge of the facility. There should be a series of ventilation shafts. That's our best option to get in."

Scott nodded, then checked the time. "Okay, let's push on."

"Eh...we may have a problem." Steph nodded her head toward Jonesy, who was lying flat on his back as if unconscious. "He's been dialing up the oxygen level to compensate for the strain of the climb. I reckon he's only got a few hours left at this rate."

"Hey, I'm dying here." Jonesy waved an arm in the air. "I never signed up for this mountain climbing shit."

"We should be there soon. Once we're inside, we won't need these suits."

"Assuming there's breathable air in there," said Steph.

"Spinner, you okay with us going on?" said Scott.

"Absolutely. Don't worry about us—we'll get the job done. Always have."

"Steph, what about just ditching these suits now, or even popping open our visors?" said Cyrus.

The doctor shook her head. "Radiation levels are lower than we thought, but I still wouldn't advise it."

"Okay, let's just push on." Scott pointed at the low-hanging clouds. "The storm is clearing. We'll lose cover in a few hours, and we need to be inside the facility before that happens."

IT TOOK a while for them to get going again, as Spinner decided to redistribute the weight between the two robotic mules so that Jonesy could use the lighter one for some support. The robots were tough and robust, and could carry a lot of gear, but not enough to allow Jonesy to simply ride on top like the miners of old would have done back in the day. But at least they were now on flat ground, so they started to make better progress.

Scott also began to feel a little less paranoid, and had stopped scanning the upper ridges for signs of movement. Nevertheless, after a while he began to notice Cyrus looking up into the cloud bank more that he reckoned was normal. He moved up beside him and switched his comm to person-to-person. "See something?"

"I'm getting trace readings on several spectra. My guess is there's a drone up there."

Scott glanced up—not that he was going to see anything. Only Cyrus's augmented vision could penetrate the thick gloom above. "Are you sure it's a drone?"

"I'm not a hundred percent, but it's got a similar signature and it's been crisscrossing back and forth over this area several times."

"You think it's spotted us?"

"With these suits on, maybe not. But those mules give off a lot of EMF—enough possibly for a drone to detect."

"Where is it now?"

"It's headed away northward at high speed."

Scott glanced up again. "Okay, let me know if it comes back."

"Will do."

"And Cyrus?"

"Yeah?"

"Let's keep it between ourselves for now."

Cyrus nodded. "Understood."

4

DRONES

I t wasn't long before the drone returned. This time they could all see it as a black dot traversing the northern sky, skimming the underside of the cloud bank. The team stood mute as they tracked it moving slowly westward until it finally disappeared back into the cloud bank.

"What was that?" Spinner's voice crackled in Scott's headset.

"Scout drone," replied Scott.

"You mean we're being hunted down?" said Jonesy.

"It's just a flyby—it doesn't mean anything." Scott tried to calm things down a bit, take the heat of Jonesy's fear so that everyone could stay focused on the mission.

"It's searching for something," said Spinner. "Maybe we were spotted before we flew into that electrical storm, and now it's trying to find us again." He was still looking up to where the drone had disappeared in the cloud bank.

"Maybe. Then again, maybe not. Let's not concern ourselves with it—we need to keep going."

One by one they started moving, cautiously glancing skyward every now and again for any sign that the scout drone had returned.

As they progressed, the landscape around them began to change. The road narrowed and twisted, and the sides rose up until they found themselves walking through a shallow canyon. Here and there, new trails would break off from the main road and wind a path up the sides of the canyon walls to what looked like entrances into old, abandoned mines. Scott wondered what creatures, if any, lurked in those dark holes in the rock. More than once he thought he saw some movement within, but kept it to himself and brushed it aside as just his paranoia.

Their progress was good, and Scott's confidence began to build as the team drew closer to the entrance of the Dyrell Labs facility. As they rounded a bend in the road, he could now make out its crumbled outline in the distance, less than a kilometer ahead.

That's when Cyrus grabbed Scott's arm. "Wait." The engineer was looking at an area of the sky almost directly overhead. "It's coming back."

"Where?" Scott looked up and scanned the cloud bank.

"Coming in fast." Cyrus turned to Scott. "We better find some cover—quick."

"Okay," said Scott as he turned back to the others. "Let's get out of sight. Over there." He pointed up to a spot on the canyon wall with a deep overhang. "We'll take cover under that until it passes."

They started running just as the drone burst out from the clouds. It banked hard and came in fast down along the route of the road, getting lower as it approached them.

Someone fired off a plasma shot.

"What the hell!" Scott stopped and looked around to see who was firing. "For God's sake, don't shoot at it."

"Why the hell not?" Jonesy was readying his weapon again just as the drone banked around and came in for another flyby.

"It's just a data drone—a scout. Now you're telling it we're a threat."

"Damn right we are." Jonesy let loose another blast just as the drone came in on a low pass. His shot struck the drone on the side and encased the machine in an incandescent blue ball of electrical craziness. It sparked and fizzled and the drone dropped out of the sky, smashing into the road a few hundred meters ahead. It bounced once, twice, and then exploded.

"Yeehaw! God dang, did you see that? I took that bitch down." Jonesy jumped and hollered.

Scott ran over to him and yanked the plasma weapon

from Jonesy's grip with such force that Jonesy lost his balance and fell over.

"You crazy bastard. Do you realize what you've done?" Scott was furious.

Jonesy rolled over, trying to pick himself up from the dirt. "Probably saved all your asses, is all. That thing could have taken us all out."

Scott jumped down on him and pinned him to the ground. He groped for the catch on Jonesy's visor as the miner tried to fight him off. Scott found the button and the visor popped open.

The miner's eyes widened and his face reconfigured into a look of horror. "What the... You trying to kill me?" He tried to close the visor, but he was pinned.

Scott aimed a punch for Jonesy's exposed face.

"Scott—no!" Steph grabbed his arm just as Cyrus and Spinner came over and tried to haul him off the stricken miner.

"Jeez, Scott. Get a grip, buddy." Cyrus grabbed Scott's other arm and pulled him off.

Scott relaxed a little and stared wild-eyed at the miner. "That was just a dumb scout drone collecting data. It would have taken hours for there to be a response to our being here. But no, you had to go shoot it down. Now it'll escalate us up to a security threat." Scott slowly stood up and took a few steps back. "You know what that means, you dumb ass? It means this place will soon be crawling with drones...and these ones will be armed. It means you could have screwed the entire mission." He kicked the ground in frustration.

"Hey, take it easy, man." Spinner held a hand up to Scott, then turned and went to help Jonesy up from the dirt.

"Yeah, well, I didn't sign up for this shit." Jonesy snapped his visor closed.

"Cool it, Jonesy." Spinner grabbed him by the shoulder and jerked a finger at his face. "Just shut the hell up for once."

Jonesy stayed quiet, but eyed Scott with extreme suspicion just in case he decided to make another go for him.

"He's right," said Spinner, turning back to Scott. "This is not what we signed up for. It was supposed to be a quick in-out job. Get you guys into the facility, that's all. Not all this Rambo shit."

"Yeah, and we want more money. Double the contract...call it danger money." Jonesy squared himself up, facing off against Scott. "Now I probably got radiation poisoning, thanks to you."

"I said cool it, Jonesy." Spinner looked like he meant business, and Jonesy backed off.

"You're fine. Levels are very low here." Steph stepped in between them, and they all took a moment to calm down.

"Look, Scott." Spinner's tone was calm. "If what you say is right, then the mission is over. I say we contact the mothership and get a rescue shuttle down here to pull us out."

Scott took a deep breath. "There is no rescue shuttle —not anymore. Your buddy here took care of that. The AI that controls this region has probably escalated the incident, so it will be operating on a security protocol now. That means nothing will be allowed in or out of here."

"What do you mean, 'no shuttle?'" Jonesy's face had a look of incredulity.

"What he means," said Cyrus, "is that when you shot down that scout drone, you changed the game."

"So, you want to go on?" said Spinner.

Scott looked over at the miner. "Even if we wanted to scrub the mission, we can't. Our shuttle is dead in the water and, according to Razzo, won't be operational for another few hours. By that time, this area will be drone central. So, we have no choice... We need to get into that facility as soon as humanly possible. Only then do we have a chance."

"Well, that's just peachy..." Jonesy was about to say more, but Spinner gave him a look that suggested he'd had just about enough of Jonesy's bullshit, and that any more would end in violence—this time from him.

"It will take us another half an hour or so to reach the entrance. The same again to get to the first of the ventilation shafts. Then it will be up to you to get us in." Scott pointed a finger at Spinner.

"How long have we got before more drones show up?" said Spinner.

"I started getting a signature from that scout drone around two hours after we dropped into Earth's atmosphere," said Cyrus. "My guess is we've got about the same: two hours, tops."

"So, we don't have any time to waste. Come on, let's keep moving." Scott turned and strode off down the road. The others followed.

CYRUS HAD MOVED up beside Scott and the two had been walking together in silence for some time. "That Jonesy guy is a goddamn liability," he eventually said.

Scott checked his comm to make sure it was on person-to-person. "Yeah, he's been a pain in the ass ever since we left Mars."

"Couldn't they have found us a better mining crew than these bozos?"

"They're the best of the best at what they do, apparently. That being digging their way in and out of places that no one else can access." Scott sighed. "The truth is, we need them, Cyrus. I know it's a pain, but we're stuck with it now."

"Jeez, he had to go and shoot down that drone."

"Just keep those eyes of yours sharp. We'll be needing them before the day's out."

Cyrus went silent for a while, periodically scanning the sky above. "It should have been a military operation."

"You're raking over old ground, Cyrus. We've been through all that. The decision was made to operate under the guise of a scientific survey mission. Less suspicious, and that drone would have simply tagged us as that."

"I know, and I get it. A military mission could have been regarded as an act of war, but..."

"But nothing." Scott stopped for a beat and looked at the engineer. "We've just had some bad luck, that's all. We can still pull this off." He moved on again.

"We can't fight off a swarm of military drones, if they come for us. We need to get out of here somehow—find a cave or an old mine and maybe hide out until the shuttle is fixed."

"I'm not giving up on this just yet. Another hour and we should be there."

"Another hour and we could all be dead."

Scott stopped again. "I'm not going to hide, Cyrus. We have to keep going. We just have to find a way."

"Scott, you and I have been through a lot of scrapes together, but this isn't about Athena, or Solomon's pan-solar QI network, or saving humanity from itself. For you this is about Miranda, isn't it?"

Scott stayed silent for a beat and lowered his head. "Now isn't the time to bring that up, Cyrus. We have a job to do."

"I bring it up because it's clouding your judgment, Scott. Christ, you nearly killed that Jonesy guy back there. I've never seen you like that."

"Yeah, I know—I lost it with him. Not good. I

shouldn't have done that." He stopped again and looked at Cyrus. "Perhaps you're right. Maybe you should take Steph and the others and find a cave to hole up in until the shuttle is back in the air. I'll take one of the mules and carry on by myself. I don't want to put any more lives at risk."

"No way, buddy. Miranda was my friend, too, and Steph's, so you're not getting out of it that easily. Going on your own is crazy. You know that, Scott. We can all still get out of this—we can come back and try another time."

"No… I'm not turning back now. I can't, Cyrus. Not when I'm so close."

But Cyrus didn't answer. The engineer was frozen on the spot, looking up at the northern sky.

Scott turned his head in the same direction, but could see nothing. "What is it?"

"Drones…two. No, wait…three. Coming in fast."

"Shit, so soon? Goddamnit, I thought we'd have more time." Scott looked around for any cover they could use, then flipped his comms to broadcast. "Drones!" he shouted, then pointed up at the canyon wall where a path led to an old mine entrance. "Up there—everybody head for that opening. We'll take cover inside."

Steph was first to respond. She ran ahead with Cyrus, one of the robotic mules following close behind.

Scott waved frantically at Spinner and Jonesy, who had lagged behind. "Move, move!"

The two miners took a second to orient themselves,

but they too were soon running for the mine entrance, with the second mule increasing its speed to match them.

They had just reached the halfway point up the winding path to the entrance when the first of the drones screamed past, then a second, and a third.

Scott glanced back to see them bank high up in the southern sky and prepare for another flyby. "Hurry, they're coming back," he shouted into his comms, and looked around to wait for the two miners to catch up.

The first of the drones completed its turn and began to fly straight at them just as Spinner raced past Scott. Jonesy was still behind, taking aim at the drone.

"Jonesy, leave it! Just get inside. Come on, hurry," Scott shouted into his comm just as the ground beside him was raked by a laser pulse. Dust filled his vision and his suit electronics flickered as it tried to mitigate the electrostatic blast that accompanied the burst of fire. His foot caught on a rock, and he stumbled face-first onto the dusty path. Scott frantically gathered himself up just as another blast of incandescent energy hit the canyon wall above him. His comm was filled with shouts and screams as he ducked in through the mine entrance.

Ahead of him, he could see Cyrus crouching behind a large boulder, weapon in hand, ready to fire. Steph, Spinner, and the mule with the EPR device were working their way in farther down the entrance.

"Where's Jonesy and the other mule?" said Cyrus as he poked his head out from behind the boulder.

Scott turned around, facing down the tunnel back

toward the opening just as Jonesy scrambled in. Behind him, Scott could see the mule—the one with all the mining equipment and explosives—making its way up to the entrance, unaware of the drama playing out around it. It was just about to cross the threshold when it was struck by a short laser burst from above.

It exploded with such force that Scott felt the impact of the shockwave like he had been hit by a small planet. He went careening down the mine entrance, tumbling and bouncing off the walls and the floor for what seemed like an eternity. When he finally stopped tumbling, he could still feel the ground shaking and trembling as the mine entrance collapsed under several tons of rock.

He tried to move, but his body didn't respond. Then his EVA suit electronics flickered and fizzled, and Scott's world went dark.

5

VANHEILDING

Fredrick VanHeilding sat comfortably in an antique leather wing-backed chair in his personal study on board the family's vast and luxurious orbital space station. It was currently parked in a geosynchronous orbit high above the central Pacific Ocean. His study was a voluminous, circular area, with most of its walls and the floor manufactured from a thick polymer glass. Through this, the gentle arc of Earth's curvature could be seen in all its glory.

He had been observing a tropical storm as it tracked its way east across the ocean. It had made landfall over the edge of the North American continent some time ago and was now beginning to dissipate. He enjoyed this simple pleasure: observing the great meteorological weather systems play out in real time, the slow and ceaseless meandering of powerful forces as they moved and shifted across the planet's surface. He found it deeply soothing, even hypnotic.

An alert flashed in the corner of his eye, by virtue of his biological lenses having been enhanced for a multitude of communications and data display. It was the orbital's AI, Marlyn.

He sighed at this intrusion into his meditations. Nevertheless, he gestured with one hand to confirm the alert and open comms. "What's so important that I need to be disturbed?" His voice did not disguise his irritation.

"Please forgive my intrusion on your meditations, sir. However, the algorithm has recently acquired new data that may be of interest to you."

VanHeilding sighed again. "Somehow I doubt it. But go on, if you must."

"Approximately three hours ago, a Belt-registered shuttle landed near a region of the Wasteland formally known as Death Valley. It was transporting a scientific survey mission."

"And I should care, why?" VanHeilding punctuated this response with yet another sigh.

"A team of five persons in full EVA suits and two robotic mules disembarked and headed on foot toward the eastern mountain range. The shuttle, however, remains in situ. We suspect it may have developed some technical issues during its descent."

"I'm going to give you three seconds to get to the point, otherwise I am terminating this conversation."

"Yes, sir. I will try to be as succinct as possible."

"Just get on with it." VanHeilding's voice rose a few decibels to signify his increasing irritation.

"The algorithm that controls this region extrapolated a risk variance level sufficient for it to deploy a scout drone to investigate this mission. Unfortunately, when this drone made contact with the team, it was shot down and destroyed."

"I can't see how this needs to be brought to my attention. Just arrest them, or eradicate them—I don't care which—and let me get back to my meditations."

"If I may, sir, there is more information that you need to be aware of. Prior to the destruction of the drone, it managed to perform a biometric scan of the party to identify the individuals. One of whom is Commander Scott McNabb, formerly of the scientific survey vessel Hermes."

This finally got VanHeilding's attention. He sat forward in his chair. "McNabb? What the—"

"He is also accompanied by two other members from that crew, namely Chief Engineer Cyrus Sanato, and Chief Medical Officer Dr. Stephanie Rayman."

VanHeilding stood up. "What the hell are they doing there?"

"Good question, sir. The algorithm escalated the incident and invoked level one security protocols, enabling it to deploy a number of security drones and a contingent of security personnel to investigate the shuttle."

"And...?"

"They have taken the pilot after a brief exchange of weapons fire. She is now in custody, undergoing interrogation in a local facility. The shuttle was extensively damaged in the firefight, however. There is a cyber-forensics team on site analyzing all information contained within what remains of the shuttle's dataset."

VanHeilding stood up and started pacing. "So, what are they doing here? What's in the Wasteland that could be of interest to them?"

"The interrogation of the pilot has revealed that their mission involves entering the old Dyrell Labs facility and reactivating the quantum intelligence known as Athena."

"What? But...that was destroyed during the Rim War. There's no way into that facility—all access has been buried under tons of rock."

"Be that as it may, that is their mission."

"But why? What do they hope to achieve?" VanHeilding was pacing furiously now.

"The algorithm has analyzed all the current data and extrapolated a likely scenario. Would you like to hear it, sir?"

"Damn right I would." He stopped pacing and moved over to the observation window, casting a glance down to the region of Earth where the storm was now clearing.

"The algorithm has postulated that Athena has not been destroyed. It still functions—at least, it has done so up until recently. This has been ascertained from the events surrounding the Europa incident. It has hypothesized that the QI, Solomon, used the original

EPR device to make contact with Athena, its original developer. So Athena was functional back then, even though the facility was assumed destroyed. Our assessment is that they intend to reestablish this superluminal connection with Solomon, and by extension the QI, Aria, and others. In effect, they are attempting to undermine the efficacy of the inter-AI network that manages all Earth-based systems."

"Holy shit, can they possibly be that stupid? Do they really think such a ludicrous plan will actually work?"

"It seems so."

VanHeilding paused for a moment and rubbed his brow, thinking. "Where are they now?"

"They were confronted by three security drones a short time ago. However, they took evasive action by utilizing one of the many mines in that area as an escape route. The mine entrance collapsed during the confrontation, so scout drones are now searching for another way in."

"They must be stopped, you hear? And if they have an EPR device with them, it must be acquired—intact."

"It will be so. Just one question, sir."

"What?"

"Our understanding is that the entity known as Scott McNabb has a significant relationship factor with your extended family by virtue of his association with Miranda Lee-VanHeilding. What outcomes would you prefer for this entity?"

"Kill him...without prejudice. And please ensure that the rest of his associates do not leave this planet alive."

"Understood, sir."

- Connection Terminated -

6

THE MINE

From the depths of the utter blackness two motes of light appeared, dancing in rhythm, growing in size and brightness. As they moved closer and closer, Scott's brain tried to make sense of this phenomenon. Was he really seeing this, or was it just in his mind—a dream perhaps, or maybe a hallucination?

The lights began to take form and shape, and soon he began to make out two ghostly figures moving toward him. They stopped and knelt beside him. He recognized their faces—Cyrus Sanato and Dr. Stephanie Rayman.

Cyrus reached out and fiddled with Scott's helmet, finally popping open his visor. Scott coughed and retched as his lungs took their first taste of the stale, dusty air.

"He's still alive," someone said. Scott wasn't sure who.

"Scott? Scott...are you injured?" This time he recognized the voice as Dr. Rayman.

He mentally examined the extremities of his body

and tentatively moved his head followed by an arm. This last action sent a wave of pain rippling down his right side. He gasped.

"Easy, buddy," said Cyrus.

"Just take it slow," said Steph.

Scott eased himself into a sitting position and rested his back against the wall, which resulted in another stab of pain rifling through his body. He clutched his ribcage, and his face contorted in pain.

"Can you feel your legs?" said Steph as she moved closer to remove his EVA suit helmet.

"Yeah, I think so."

"Does that hurt?" Steph poked at the ribs on the right side of his body.

Scott yelled.

"I'll take that as a yes," she said. "You've got a couple broken ribs there. Looks like that EVA suit took most of the blast. Can you stand up?"

"Yeah, maybe. Can you give me a hand?" Again, pain rifled down his right side as Scott tried to move. Cyrus and Steph came to either side of him and grabbed an arm each, helping him up off the floor of the mine entrance and into a standing position. He gasped several times as the pain in his broken ribs made itself known.

"Shit, what a mess." He clutched his ribs.

"You need to get out of that EVA suit. I can bandage your ribs and give you something for the pain, but that's the most I can do."

Scott looked up and tried to see around him, but it

was difficult as the space was dark, and dust filled the air. "Spinner? Jonesy?"

Steph and Cyrus looked from one to the other. "Jonesy's dead," Steph finally said. "He was crushed by falling rock when the entrance caved in."

"Goddamnit." Scott shook his head. "I shouted at him to hurry, but he just kept on shooting at that drone." He reached up and rubbed his skull. "And Spinner, is he all right?"

"He's okay, sort of."

"What do you mean, 'sort of?'"

"He was farther down the entrance tunnel, so he escaped most of the blast, but…he's taking Jonesy's death pretty bad."

Scott lowered his head and sighed. "Where is he now?"

"Up near the entrance, sitting beside the body," said Steph as she began to help him out of the EVA suit.

"I better go and check on him," said Cyrus, who walked off toward the entrance. "What are the radiation levels like in here, Steph? I feel a bit exposed with no suit."

"Fine for the moment. And it's probably a lot less if we move farther in."

"Did the quantum device survive?"

"Cyrus thinks it's okay, and the mule survived, too. Just as well, because it was carrying this medical kit." Steph knelt and broke out a syringe from the kit as she spoke. She cracked open the seal and jabbed it into Scott's side. "This will help reduce the pain."

It took a few more minutes for Scott to gather himself together and put the EVA suit back on. He left his helmet visor open, and the suit powered down. He did not want to use any more of its resources than necessary. When they had finished, the two of them slowly made their way back up to the entrance.

CYRUS WAS SITTING BESIDE SPINNER, who cradled Jonesy's head in his lap. Cold, dead eyes looked up at them through a tangled mass of hair and blood.

Spinner glanced up as Scott and Steph came over. "We were going to open a bar, you know...back in Jezero City...from the money out of this gig." He looked back down at the face of his now dead friend.

Scott didn't know what to say. What could he say? Nothing that would do any good, that was for sure. He just sighed and looked at the looming wall of rock blocking the entrance to the mine. "We'll have to dig ourselves out of here."

"Not a chance," said Spinner.

"Why not?" said Cyrus.

"Because there's just too much rock, and a good deal of it is too big for us to move without machines."

Cyrus stood up and moved over to the wall of rock, casting the light from his helmet across its surface. "We have to try."

"If we had some equipment, then sure, no problem," said Spinner. "But all our gear was destroyed when the mule blew up." He looked up at them. "Trust me, this is what I do—moving rock—and there's no way we can dig our way out of here."

"Then we'll just have to find another way out," said Scott as he turned on his helmet's light and looked back down the tunnel.

It took some time to get themselves together, and for the realization to finally sink in that there was simply no way back out through the entrance. They were trapped inside the old mine, and the only option was to find another exit. Since no one knew how long that would take—or if they would find one at all—they eventually agreed to shut down their EVA suits and breathe the air in the mine. It was stale and dusty, but the radiation levels were low, and getting lower as they moved farther into the mine.

However, this meant they couldn't use their heads-up for low-light environments, as this was integrated into the visor. And since they needed the visor open so they could breathe, they now had to rely on old-fashioned lights to see where they were going. Except for Cyrus; his augmented vision allowed him full clarity in almost complete darkness, so he took the lead. Fortunately, the quantum device had survived the drone attack unscathed, along with the robotic mule, so there was that, at least.

Spinner had been reluctant to leave the body of his

colleague just lying on the dusty floor—abandoned, so to speak—and it took both Scott and Steph some time to persuade him that they had no other option. What finally persuaded Spinner in the end was Scott's suggestion that he could stay with the body while the others looked for a way out. If and when they found one, they would come back for him. This seemed to trigger Spinner's survival instincts, and so he reckoned he had a better chance by sticking with them.

They moved slowly and in silence, each lost in their own thoughts. For Scott, it was clear that the mission was turning out to be a disaster. Jonesy was dead, and all the equipment they would need to gain access to the facility where Athena was situated had been destroyed. As for the shuttle, all his attempts to raise Razzo on comms were met with static. Either the transmission could not penetrate the tons of rock that surrounded him, or the shuttle had been found by a scout drone and possibly destroyed. In his heart, he hoped that the former was the more likely scenario.

For Scott and the team, the reality was that they were trapped inside a labyrinthine mine, running low on resources, with little hope of escape. There was now absolutely no prospect of achieving the mission objective. At best, all they could hope for was survival, and even that seemed tenuous. The only upside, if you could call it that, was that the drones couldn't pursue them into the mine.

.   .   .

THE TUNNEL WAS low and narrow, so they moved in single file. Cyrus took the lead, with Steph and Spinner behind. Scott took up the rear, with the mule following along. Every now and again, the tunnel would widen a little, with alcoves on either side. The first time they encountered these they had hoped it might be an intersection, but it was not to be. For the most part, the tunnel stayed straight and true, descending farther and farther into the mountain.

They had walked for around a kilometer or so—Scott wasn't really sure—when the tunnel widened dramatically and they found themselves entering a huge natural cave. They stopped, casting the light from their helmets around the cavern. Great, broad stalactites dropped down from above, and some had even joined up with their corresponding stalagmites to form natural columns.

The path they were on seemed to skirt the western edge of the cavern, disappearing again into another tunnel on the far side. As Scott moved his head to peer into the cavernous blackness, he glimpsed a reflection. He moved in farther to examine it and slowly began to realize that he was looking at a large, freshwater pond.

"Check this out—water," he shouted out to the others.

Cyrus came over and stood beside him. "Well, at least we won't die of thirst."

"I wouldn't count on it. That water could be highly toxic." Steph moved past them and around the edge of the pond. She stopped suddenly, knelt, and waved back to the others. "Have a look at this."

Scott and Cyrus came over and examined the area of the ground that had caught Steph's attention. There, imprinted in the soft, sandy soil of the cave floor, was a set of human footprints.

"Ho-ly shit," said Cyrus.

Scott knelt to examine them. "How old are these?" It was more a question to himself.

"They're recent." Spinner now joined them, and seemed to be pretty certain of his assessment of the footprints' age.

"How do you know?"

He knelt and pointed to one of the prints. "The sand here is very fine and dry." He picked up a handful and let it spill out from between his fingers. "See the sharpness at the edges of the impressions? These would round out over time, with dust falling and slight air droughts coming in from the mine entrance. But these are well-defined, which makes me think they're recent."

"How recent?"

"A few months, maybe. Hard to say." He stood up and scanned the area. "My guess is that one person, or maybe two, came in from over there somewhere." He pointed off into the gloom of the cavern. "They moved across these rocks, down to this sandy patch, and over to the edge of the pond. You can see here that they spent some time moving around." Spinner pointed to a confused, trampled area. "Then moved off again, back the same way."

"Maybe they were getting water?" said Cyrus.

"Possibly," said Steph. "If so, then this might be okay to drink."

Scott considered Spinner's analysis of the footprints for a moment, then moved out of the sandy area and up onto a low, rocky outcrop. He scanned the gloom with his helmet light.

"See anything?" said Cyrus.

"Not really. Just more cave." Scott stepped down and rejoined the others. "Okay, we could keep going on the path we came in on, follow it around to that exit over there, and see where it leads us." He pointed off to the opposite side of the cavern. "Or we could try to follow these footprints and see if it leads to another way out."

"Well, if there's someone else here, wouldn't they be worth finding?" said Steph.

"That depends," said Spinner.

"On what?" said Steph.

"On whether they want to be found."

"It doesn't matter if they do or they don't. I think it's still our best chance of finding a way out." Scott turned toward the blackness at the far end of the cave. "So, if they came in from over there, then that's where we have to go."

They all stood in silence for a moment, looking into the darkness, their thoughts only broken by the sound of the robotic mule as it clattered its way over beside them.

Scott turned around to look at it. "Well, it looks like we're all here, so let's get going. The sooner we find this person, the sooner we get out of here."

They moved off into the darkness, sweeping their lights across the way ahead. Soon they began to make out the walls and roof of the cavern as it narrowed. The path became flat and sandy, and here and there they picked up the impressions of disturbances in the dust. The route they found themselves on now had a clear pattern beaten into it. People had passed this way before, but how long ago was hard to tell.

The cavern narrowed further and became a long, winding tunnel. Natural—not made by human hands, but by the forces of nature. The base and sides were smooth and curved, with clearly visible layers of sediment laid down over the eons. Scott reckoned that it must have been an underground river at some point in the very distant past.

They found more signs of human activity: numbers and letters scratched on the walls and the rock. Not words, as such. More like codes or identifying marks perhaps made a long time ago by those who worked the mines here—or were they more recent? Again, it was hard to tell. Yet apart from the clear footprints at the edge of the lake in the first cave, they had seen little else in the way of hard evidence that someone was occupying this cave system. Still, there were hints and clues here and there: the beaten path, the markings on the walls, disturbances in the soil that were clearly made by human activity.

They made slow progress, mostly because they all concentrated on trying to penetrate the darkness to search for clues, sweeping their helmet lights around, trying to pick out something that could give them hope that they might find a way out.

Their progress was further hampered by Spinner, who had grown more detached and sullen, and now seldom spoke. He would lag behind, as if each step required a Herculean effort on his part. Sometimes he would simply stop and stare at the ground, lost in his grief and emotional trauma. Scott, for his part, could not bring himself to play the tough leader and kick Spinner's ass to get him moving again. He had lost his friend, whose broken and battered body now lay dead at the mouth of the mine, so Scott just didn't have it in him to compound the miner's misery. Instead, it was left to Dr. Rayman's more practiced bedside manner to coax Spinner out of his paralysis and continue on with the search.

They had moved along in this torturous stop-start manner for some time when the tunnel finally widened and opened out into yet another vast cavern. So big that their helmet lights were barely able to perceive its depth in the darkness. The air changed, too, becoming cooler and less stale, and there was a hint of something vaguely botanical.

Scott found himself taking deep, satisfying breaths.

"The air feels fresh here," he said as he took another deep breath. "Could be coming in from outside somewhere. What's the radiation level like, Steph?"

She checked her monitor, tapping on some icons to perform a detailed analysis. "Virtually nonexistent."

"Is that not a bit strange?" said Scott. "This air must be coming from outside the cave system, which means we should be seeing a rise in radiation levels."

Cyrus stood in front and scanned the cave from left to right. He raised a hand to signal them to stop moving. "Everyone, wait up."

"What is it?" Scott whispered.

"People—lots of them. I count fifteen, maybe twenty."

Scott moved his helmet light across the cavern, but he could see nothing but stalagmites. He noticed that Steph and Spinner were doing the same. "I can't see anyone," he whispered again.

"They're hiding in the darkness, but I see them. I'm detecting their heat signatures on infrared. Also...they're armed."

"Shit." Scott delicately unclipped the plasma pistol strapped to his right thigh. The others did the same. "What are they doing, Cyrus?"

"Nothing at the moment. Just waiting. I don't think they realize we can see them. And I don't think they're security personnel."

"How come?" Scott flicked the safety off on his weapon.

"Their weapons are ancient ballistic guns."

"Seriously? Gunpowder?"

"As far as I can tell."

Steph slowly moved up beside them. "What do we do?"

"I think—" But Scott's sentence was cut short by a barrage of bright, incandescent light that burst out from the blackness. He instinctively raised an arm to shield his eyes from the intense brightness. As his brain slowly recalibrated his vision to accommodate the dramatically increased light level, Scott began to see ghostly figures move out from the shadows and surround them on all sides. As his eyes adjusted more, and the figures moved farther into the light, he realized that this was a ragtag group of civilians. Dirty and dusty, thin and gaunt— almost feral. They all carried ancient ballistic weapons, which were deadly nonetheless, and they were all aimed directly at them.

A voice broke out from the throng. "If you want to keep living, then I suggest you stop right there. Nobody move."

7

SHIN-AU-AV

S cott's brain frantically tried to assess the threat level. It was clear that this group wasn't military, so that was something. But that didn't mean they were friendly, either, judging by the number of weapons aimed at them. He fought off the instinct to raise the plasma pistol he held in his right hand, just in case it might spook some trigger-happy member of this ragtag tribe. Instead he raised his left hand in a gesture of submission—a gesture to indicate that nobody should do anything stupid.

A member of the group slowly emerged from the shadows and stood between two bright floodlights. He was a heavyset, middle-aged man, clean-shaven with tightly cropped hair. Unlike the others, he carried a sophisticated plasma weapon, but still had it slung over his shoulder. On either side of him, two more figures emerged and kept pace; both had ballistic weapons aimed threateningly at Scott and the crew.

The figure stopped a few meters ahead and looked each of them over with a curious eye. "I take it you guys are not from around here?"

Scott took a cautious step forward. "Eh...yeah, we're a scientific survey team and we're...eh...lost."

"Survey teams don't usually shoot down scout drones."

"That was a mistake," said Scott. "It wasn't intentional."

"Really? Well, just so there are no more *mistakes,* I want you to—very gently—place all your weapons on the ground and then back away...slowly."

Scott carefully lowered his pistol to the ground and turned around to ensure that the rest of the crew was also going to comply. The way he saw it, they had no choice but to do what they were asked. Cyrus and Steph were already depositing their weapons on the cave floor, but to Scott's dismay, he could see Spinner crouched behind the robotic mule, his plasma weapon in hand, ready to fire.

He raised a hand to him. "Spinner, just put it down."

"No way." Spinner's eyes darted this way and that. "I'm staying right here."

The mood in the cave changed noticeably. Scott could hear people shifting position and more weapons being drawn. He raised his other hand and stepped in front of Spinner. "Take it easy. This isn't going to help."

The miner said nothing, just gripping the weapon tighter. Scott started to get the feeling that this was not going to end well. He really didn't care if Spinner got himself killed in a shootout. Sure, it would be tragic—pointless, even. But he could live with it. However, what he did care about was a stray bullet damaging the quantum device strapped to the mule that Spinner was using as cover.

"Spinner...it's okay." Steph moved over and placed a hand on the muzzle of the miner's weapon. He looked up at her, and slowly the fight leaked out of him. He lowered the weapon and placed it on the ground. There was an audible sigh of relief in the cavern, and the group relaxed a little.

Their leader stepped in closer. "Now if you'd all just move back a few paces, that would be great."

Scott and the crew did as they were told, and several of the ragtag group moved forward to pick up the weapons. Now that they were disarmed and no longer a threat, Scott ventured a request. "Look, all we need is just to find another way out of here. Can you help us?"

But his request was ignored. Instead he was grabbed on both sides, his arms twisted behind his back, and his wrists tied together with cable. He heard the shouts of protest from the others as they were all subjected to the same treatment. Their helmets were then forcibly removed, and Scott felt the muzzle of a weapon shoved into his back, prodding him to start walking. All the lights suddenly extinguished, and Scott found himself completely disoriented until he began to pick out dim illumination emanating from lights that each of the group seemed to carry.

He started walking, following behind what seem to be a long line of people. Several times he tried to look back and see where the others were, but each time he was poked in the back, and couldn't find out where they were or how they were holding up.

As they walked, he estimated the size of the group to be upward of twenty members. Their clothes were lightweight and utilitarian, with a lot of belts and pockets. He noticed, too, that they all had face masks or scarves that they used to cover their mouths and noses. He realized that this group must live in these caves, and there were probably a great many more. None of the reconnaissance data that Scott and the team had studied before the mission had given any indication of people living anywhere in the Wasteland. In fact, it was presumed that no humans existed for at least a million square kilometers. Yet here was a population eking out an existence in the caves and mines, safe from radiation, undetected. Were there more groups like this? Or was this just an isolated population?

These and many other questions percolated in Scott's brain as he made his way along a maze of paths and tunnels, with a helpful prod in the back every now and again from the business end of a ballistic weapon.

They had twisted and turned their way through this subterranean system for what seemed like half an hour when Scott started to see evidence of recent engineering.

Ducting and cabling ran along the walls and overhead illumination would activate automatically as they moved. He could also feel the blast of cool, fresh air being dispensed by vents placed periodically in the overhead ducting. It was becoming clear to him that they must have a significant source of energy somewhere to power all this infrastructure. But it was another half hour before they came to the first serious piece of heavy engineering: a three-meter-diameter airlock which terminated a short tunnel they had just entered. Scott recognized this airlock as the same one used on a standard interplanetary cargo transport. They must have scavenged it, disassembled it, and re-engineered it to fit this space.

The outer door cracked open and the first group of fifteen, including Scott, marched in. As they shifted and sorted themselves inside the airlock, Scott caught a glimpse of Cyrus. The two exchanged a glance. Cyrus nodded, and then gestured with his eyes around the airlock. Scott could see that he was impressed with the engineering.

Before the outer door shut, Scott looked back to see Steph with Spinner close beside her. He was also relieved to see the mule, still fully laden, tagging along beside them. The outer door shut, and the airlock began to recycle the air. One by one, the members of the group started removing face masks and scarves, and they all began to noticeably relax. Scott got the impression that whatever lay beyond the inner doors of this airlock served as home to this group, and they eagerly awaited it.

.   .   .

WHEN THE INNER doors finally opened, Scott was surprised by what he saw. It wasn't quite what he had been expecting. He had imagined more of the same—dusty tunnels and dark, gloomy caverns—but this was different. The doors opened out onto a sleek, wide, manmade platform. What happened next was even more surprising: it started to descend down a smooth-walled shaft. The descent was short, perhaps fifty meters or so. Finally, another set of well-engineered doors opened to reveal what could only be described as a subterranean city built inside a vast, domed cavern. Scott stood in wonder for a moment and then had to remind himself that he was not in one of the colonies of the outer worlds, but on Earth itself.

From their elevated position on the airlock platform, he could see down and across the floor of a cavern that seemed to go on forever. The entire space, as far as he could tell, was covered in lush, green vegetation. The sides of the cavern sloped upward and were cut into stepped terraces, most of which were also covered in vegetation. But what surprised him the most were the buildings.

All around the upper terraces were structures built from cut stone. They had arched windows and doors, two or three stories tall, all interspersed with domes and turrets. It was clearly the work of some long-lost civilization that had to predate the current occupants by many hundreds—if not thousands—of years.

The cavern floor was also dotted with similar

buildings, but these had been augmented by newer structures made with modern materials: plastics, metal, concrete. Above him, the entire space was illuminated by a constellation of lights that seemed to be suspended midway between the floor and the roof of the cavern. There also looked to be hundreds of people living and working in the space. All this Scott took in during the few moments he had been standing on the platform while the rest of the group piled out of the airlock.

Soon he was again being poked in the ribs and moved onward. They took a path along the edge of a terrace for a short distance, past several of the cut-stone buildings. The craftsmanship was superb, with barely a gap between each of the stones. It reminded him of images he had seen of the Inca site Machu Picchu. The ancient age of the stones was further evidenced by the size and number of lichens growing over their surfaces.

They were finally ushered into one of these buildings not far from where they had entered the cavern. From the outside, Scott had assumed it to be small and narrow, but once he entered, he could see that it was just a facade for a much larger space that had been hacked out from the side of the cavern. It seemed to be a barracks of some kind, with stores and equipment stacked here and there. They passed through a number of locked doors until finally he was shoved into an empty stone room along with Cyrus, Steph, and Spinner. One of the group began to untie their wrists while the others kept their weapons trained on them.

Their leader stood in the doorway and, after a few moments, began to speak. "My name is Tugo, and I am the leader of this contingent. Your actions in shooting down that scout drone have caused us problems...so much so that we cannot allow you to go wandering around, either in the cave system or outside."

"So what, then?" Scott rubbed his wrists. "You're just going to lock us up here?"

"For the moment, yes. We need to discuss what to do with you."

"You can't get away with this. We're a Belt-sponsored science team—people will be looking for us."

Tugo ignored him. "I need you all to get out of those EVA suits. You won't be needing them in here."

"Why can't you just help us on our mission?" Scott tried to sound reasonable.

"Hard and all as this may be for you to understand, we are actually helping you. So just do as I say. I will see to it that some food and water is brought in to you later." He turned and left the room.

Again, Scott was having difficulty gauging the threat level. What did he mean by saying he was "helping" them? At the same time, if they didn't comply with the request to remove their EVA suits then Scott didn't doubt violence would ensue. In the end, what choice did they have?

TWENTY MINUTES LATER, the four of them stood in the

middle of the room while all their gear was bundled up and carried out. Fortunately, they still retained the suit's thermal inner layer, so at least they wouldn't freeze. Scott lowered himself to the floor. He was exhausted from all the walking and climbing he had been doing over the last few hours. *How long has it been since we left the shuttle?* He couldn't tell; he had lost all track of time.

"Ho-ly shit," said Cyrus as he tried to rub some feeling back into his arms. "What the hell is this place?"

"I think it's Shin-Au-Av," said Steph as she sat down on the floor with her back against the wall.

"Shin—what?" Cyrus also sat down on the floor opposite.

"It's a legend," said Steph. "A mythical place."

"It looks pretty real to me," said Scott.

"Jonesy would have loved to see this place." Spinner had also collapsed on the floor.

"So, what now?" said Cyrus.

"We wait," said Scott. "Maybe we can convince them to help us. There's not much else we can do."

"They're not sure what to do with us," said Steph. "Our 'activities' have caused them some trouble."

"You mean, they're deciding whether to kill us or not?" said Cyrus.

Steph nodded. "Something like that."

Scott felt exhausted. Maybe his notion of getting help from this group was just fantasy. In reality, maybe he was a dead man who just didn't know it. Perhaps they all were. Yet he had no fight left; all he wanted to do was sleep. He slumped down on the hard stone floor.

They were all quiet for a moment, lost in their own thoughts, when Steph started to talk. "Before we came on this mission, I did a lot of research on this area," she said in a low, tired voice. "Apparently, long before the old Europeans came here, the original inhabitants of this region had a legend that spoke of a lost civilization living in a great subterranean city. They called it Shin-Au-Av."

"You mean this place?" said Cyrus.

"The story, as far as I can remember," she continued, "is that the wife of a great tribal leader died, and he was so distraught that he exiled himself from the real world and ventured into the underground world of the dead in search of her."

Scott got an uneasy feeling about this story. Somehow it seemed to parallel his deep, primal desire to be reunited with Miranda. He shifted a little on the stone floor and tried to rest.

Steph went on. "The great chief journeyed through tunnels and caverns and caves, bravely fighting off demons and monsters until, at last, he came to a bottomless gorge spanned by a narrow stone bridge. When he crossed it, he entered a fabulous land full of happy, dancing people. Some of them he recognized as dead members of his tribe, so he knew his true love must be there, and he started to search for her."

Steph looked over at Scott for a brief moment before resuming the story. "One of the people of this land decided to help the chief, and soon he and his wife were reunited. But, as always with these stories, there is a sting in the tale. Apparently, he was told he could leave with his wife, but they must not look back."

"Don't tell me," said Cyrus. "Let me guess, they looked back?"

"Yup—his wife did. As soon as she looked back, she disappeared into thin air."

"Typical," said Spinner. "Always someone who messes up a good plan."

Steph gave him a look, then carried on with the story. "The chief eventually made it back to his tribe, and his story became legend."

"Interesting story, Steph," said Scott. "You reckon this is the same place as in the legend?"

"So, you're saying we're in the land of the dead," said Cyrus.

"Well, it's just a legend," said Steph. "However, there's a bit more to the story." She shifted her position and leaned in a little. "Apparently, during the early part of the twentieth century, a couple of miners working in this region stumbled into a vast underground cavern, full of artifacts of some ancient civilization. They found mummified bodies, eight or nine feet tall, along with strange carvings and tools. But, of course, they could never find it again."

"So it was just a load of bullshit?" said Spinner.

"That's what most people thought. Yet that started off

several expeditions to find this ancient city. Needless to say, no one ever did."

"So you think this is that place, Shin—whatever?"

"Shin-Au-Av," Steph corrected. "It sure fits the bill."

"Just those buildings on their own would take decades to construct." Cyrus jerked a thumb toward the door. "These guys couldn't have built all that on their own."

Scott shifted his weight again to eke some comfort out of the stone. "None of that matters, anyway. The real question is: will they help us?"

8

INTERROGATION

Scott woke to sharp, stabbing pain in his ribs. He opened his eyes to see a guard standing over him, who proceeded to give him another kick. There wasn't much force behind it—more of a poke with his foot. But he did manage to find the spot on Scott's body where his ribs were broken.

"Wake up, they want you. Come on." The guard seemed disinterested, like it was a task he'd rather not be doing.

Scott rubbed his face and shifted his tired body into a sitting position. His ribcage ached, and he had to take a moment for the pain to subside. He glanced around the room and realized that he was alone. "Where are the others? What have you done with them?"

"They're fine. Don't worry about them. Let's get going —you're next." The guard stepped back a little as Scott rose to his feet.

"They better be, or there will be hell to pay."

"Yeah, yeah...come on." He gave Scott a push in the back to get him moving toward the door.

He was taken to an area within the same building complex, though this one had a little more infrastructure. A long wooden table with a number of benches around it took up the center of the room. The room itself was sparse, save for some overhead lighting and what looked like a retinal scanner beside the main door. Three people sat on one of the benches along one side of the table. Two men and one woman, and all looked to be middle-aged. Scott recognized the central figure as Tugo, the leader of the group that had overwhelmed them in the cave. A disheveled holo-tablet sat in the middle of the table, currently projecting a 3D rendering of the local topography.

Tugo switched it off as Scott entered. "Take a seat." He gestured to a bench on the opposite side of the table.

Scott sat down, and the guard that had escorted him left the room. The mood was calm, almost relaxed.

Tugo then gestured to either side of him. "This is Esa, and this is Adsa, and what all three of us would like to know is what the hell you guys are doing so far from home."

"What have you done with the others?" Scott was keen to get straight to the point.

"Your comrades are fine, so don't go worrying about them," Tugo replied with an irritated wave of the hand.

"So where are they?" Scott persisted.

Tugo raised a pointed finger. "We're asking the questions here. So settle down, Commander McNabb." He said Scott's name like an accusation. "So," he continued, "care to tell us what you're doing in this neck of the woods?"

Scott sighed. "We're just a science team."

"Doing what, exactly?" The woman on the left, Esa, leaned back as she spoke.

"We're collecting data on the biology of the region, studying how lifeforms develop in a high-radiation environment."

"So, you're an off-world science team searching for signs of life on Earth. Any idea how ridiculous that sounds?" They started laughing.

"That's not what I said." Scott was beginning to get irritated. "Knowing how plants behave in an irradiated environment is very useful in terms of crop production on planets without a magnetosphere."

Tugo grunted. "Perhaps. But here's the thing: it's complete bullshit, isn't it?"

Scott stayed silent.

"There's no record of a science team operating in this region." Adsa had taken up the baton now. "So, whatever it was you guys were up to, you had no authorization. That's why that drone was sent in."

"Like I said, we're just collecting data," Scott finally said.

Tugo sat back and considered Scott for a moment. "So why did you shoot it down?"

Scott sighed again. "That was a mistake."

"Damn right it was." Adsa leaned across the table as if he was about to attack Scott.

Tugo placed a hand on Adsa's shoulder and gently pulled him back. He sat down again.

"Hey, I agree—it was stupid. Jonesy...he got spooked. Started taking potshots at it, and somehow he managed to hit it." Scott shook his head.

"You have no idea, do you," said Esa, "about what you started by shooting down that drone."

"Well, it did seem to take it rather badly, since it sent a load of its buddies after us."

"We know all about that." Tugo leaned in again. "Here's the thing, Commander: those security drones don't give up. They're still out there, and they're going to hunt you down for as long as it takes." He sat back. "If not for us, you and your team would all be dead. So why don't you cut the crap and tell us what a bunch of off-worlders are doing poking around in the Wasteland?"

"I keep telling you, we're a science team."

Tugo sighed.

"So where are you from? Who's funding this...science mission?" Esa asked.

"It's an expedition co-funded by the Belt and Mars."

"Since when did the Belt and Mars become such good buddies?" she asked with a vague sneer.

Scott just shrugged his shoulders. "Who knows."

"There's no way the algo would allow any kind of off-world expedition down here, so we know you're talking crap. There's no point in trying to convince us otherwise," said Adsa.

"The algo… What's that?" Scott was genuinely unsure of what this meant.

"The algorithm. It's the AI that controls everything here," Adsa continued. "There's no way it would sanction such a mission."

Scott realized that they were no experts in interrogation. He could keep his story up all day long and they would never find a way through. But who were these people? They clearly knew the area intimately, as well as the machinations of the "algorithm," as they called it. The risk for Scott, of course, was he knew very little about who they were and, more importantly, what they stood for, if anything. So, could he trust them with the truth? Yet if Scott had any hope of achieving the mission objective, then they could potentially be of enormous help.

"Look, we can go on and on like this forever. But it's still going to be the same answer. And while we appreciate you getting us out of a jam back in the cave system, I really don't appreciate being incarcerated and prevented from continuing with our mission. So why don't we all just shake hands and we can go on our merry way?"

"Two reasons why that's not going to happen," said Tugo. "One, you guys wouldn't survive for more than ten minutes outside in the Wasteland. The drones would find you, and you would all die in a hailstorm of laser fire." He leaned forward and gestured with his hands. "Not that we really care that much if you live or die, but what we *do not* like is the increased drone activity that this scenario would lead to. Which brings me to the second reason.

"You have brought yourselves to the attention of the algorithm, and it is not going to be satisfied by simply killing you all. Like us, it wants to know what you're doing here. And let's be clear: it knows you're not here to collect data on creosote bushes and tumbleweeds.

"If you were to venture outside again, the algo would be sniffing your charred remains to glean any bit of data it could, and data is what it feeds on—it has an insatiable appetite for data. Now that you've managed to move it up to operating on a security protocol, it'll leave no stone unturned to figure out what you lot were doing here."

He gestured to his associates. "Our hope is that by holding you here, the algo will be satisfied that you all died in the explosion at the mine entrance and will scale down its operations. But this is looking increasingly unlikely. New drones have already entered the territory, adding to the search.

"This puts our future here in a difficult position, Commander McNabb. For a great many years, we have lived and prospered in this subterranean city, completely hidden from the gaze of the algorithm. We have our ways of avoiding detection by the scout drones that regularly fly over this region. But security drones are a different thing entirely, particularly ones that are hell-bent on finding answers.

"You see, we live off-grid as free people. And to be off-grid—not connected to the data networks, and by extension the algorithm—is illegal, punishable by death. So, Commander McNabb, what you and your team of bozos have instigated means that we are now in a fight for our very survival."

Tugo sat back, almost slumping into the seat as he did. His mood was sanguine, also reflected in the body language of his associates. To Scott, he had the look of someone who was facing a difficult task and, in that sense, Scott could empathize with their predicament. *If only we had stayed with the shuttle*, Scott told himself. *Maybe things would have been different.*

"There was a shuttle that we came down in." Scott's voice was low and solemn. "It was damaged during the flight through the electrical storm. We had to abandon it, and the pilot was left to try to fix it. Do you know if it's still there?"

Esa shook her head. "Sorry, they came for it. A VanHeilding shuttle landed a short time ago with a number of security personnel. There was a shootout. Your pilot survived, but she has been taken prisoner by them, no doubt for interrogation."

Scott lowered his head. "Shit."

Again, Esa shook her head. "Whatever your pilot knows, then we have to assume that the algorithm will soon know, too. So, we would really like to find out what we're up against here."

It was as Scott feared: even though Kyah Razzo didn't

know the true nature of the mission, it wouldn't take the algorithm long to figure it out. There was no other option now in Scott's mind but to come clean with this group, tell them about their plan to integrate Athena into the pan-solar QI network, and try to get their help in accomplishing it.

But first he needed to talk to the rest of the team, make sure they were all okay, and that they all agreed to this course of action. He leaned in again and rested his arms on the table. "Let me see my team first, then we can talk again. There may be a way out of this for both of us."

None of them said anything for a moment; they simply sat passively and considered him. Finally, Tugo sat forward. "Very well then. But no more bullshit."

Scott nodded.

Esa tapped her earpiece and spoke in a language that Scott didn't recognize. A few moments later, the guard entered and they all rose. Just as Scott was about to follow the guard out, Tugo came around from the other side of the table and looked him in the eye. "Just so you know, time is not on our side. So, if you have something, we want to hear it sooner rather than later."

Scott nodded and followed the guard out of the room.

9

THE COUNCIL

S cott was relieved to find all the others waiting for him when he returned to the holding cell. They had all been interrogated, in one form or another, by different members of the tribe. But none had revealed the true nature of the mission. They had stuck to the line that they were a scientific mission collecting data on the biology of the region. Even Spinner, to his credit, stuck to the script. Yet their collective mood became somber when Scott broke the news that the shuttle had been commandeered and the pilot, Kyah Razzo, taken by VanHeilding personnel.

"The way I see it," said Scott, after their initial discussions had subsided, "is that we need to persuade these people to help us. It's the only way we can salvage this mission now."

"While I get the impression they don't want to do us

any physical harm," said Cyrus, "actually helping us might be asking too much."

"We don't even know anything about them," said Steph. "We don't know who they are, where they came from, or what their ideology might be."

"One thing is for certain: they don't like AI, or the 'algorithm' that they keep going on about. Which puts us both on the same page. So, I say we come clean and tell them that our mission is to subvert the algorithm. They have to buy into that."

"Maybe," said Cyrus.

"It's also pretty obvious that they know every nook and cranny in these mountains. If there's a way into that facility, then they'll know it. I'm certain of that."

"But it's risky," said Cyrus. "If word gets out that a pan-solar alliance is trying to undermine Earth-based AI, then everything goes into lockdown. It'll be extremely difficult to get anywhere near *any* QI here on Earth after that."

"They probably already know, now that they have Razzo," said Scott.

"In that case, I don't see that we have any other option," said Steph.

"And what if they don't help us?" said Spinner. "What happens then? Are we stuck here forever, with no way off the planet? Living like troglodytes?"

"We could always try to escape," said Cyrus. "They have fairly primitive technology here; they're not that sophisticated. We would still need to get our EVA suits back, and the mule with the quantum device. But I don't figure it would be too difficult to sneak out of here, considering I can see in the dark and they can't."

"And then what?" said Steph. "We wander around in the caves like we did before?"

"There's got to be a way out," said Cyrus.

"Okay, Cyrus, I hear you. But let's call that Plan B for the moment," said Scott. "My gut feeling is that no matter what way we slice and dice this, the best option is to get them working for us, helping us get into that facility. However, if we are going to persuade them, then we'll have to give them the full story. We're here to undermine the algorithm—that should be music to their ears."

EVENTUALLY, after some further back and forth, they all agreed to take the risk of exposing the mission plan to the tribe. It was their only real option. So, after a few minutes of Scott banging on the inside of the door and hollering for some attention, a guard finally came and opened it.

"Tell Tugo that we're ready to talk turkey."

The guard was sullen, like he had been disturbed during some more important task. He replied with an imperceptible nod, and pushed Scott back inside as he closed the door and it locked again. They waited. It didn't take long; less than ten minutes later, the door swung open, and Tugo entered flanked by four guards. He gestured to them. "Let's go."

They were brought to the same room that Scott had

been interrogated in earlier, but this time there were at least a dozen people waiting for them. The room felt crowded. A bench was moved against the back wall, and they were instructed to take a seat. In front of them, around a dozen or so members of the tribe sat on three sides of a long wooden table. It reminded Scott of the painting he once saw of *The Last Supper* by Leonardo da Vinci.

The previous time he had been here, he hadn't taken much notice of the room. Now though, he could see that it was more ornate than he had first realized. The walls were made of cut stone in a complex, geometric pattern. Above the doors and windows, the sills were engraved with strange symbols and decorative flourishes. The floor was an intricately patterned mosaic, worn and dusty.

The group jostled and murmured as they organized themselves on one side of the table. There was a mix of both men and women, and all seemed to be of a similar age—not old, but not young, either. They had a similar look, too: thin, sinewy, their faces almost gaunt, and a pallid complexion, presumably as a result of living underground in the absence of natural sunlight. Their clothes were old and worn, patched and repaired several times over, their shoes a mix of repaired boots with soles made from the recycled tires of antique wheeled vehicles.

Scott tried to gauge the hierarchy of this group by the way they were arranged around the table, but it was hard to tell. Tugo sat three from the center, and Scott wondered if the power structure radiated out from the central pair, with the least important people at the end of the table. It might have seemed like a minor observation, but in Scott's mind it was important that he could identify the leader of the group. This would be the person he ultimately needed to persuade.

Eventually, after much shuffling and sorting, a hand was raised by an older woman who sat at the very edge of the group. The others fell silent as she turned to Scott and the crew. "I am Padooa. We are ready. You may begin."

This threw Scott a bit. Was she the leader, or was it someone else? Then a thought struck him: maybe they didn't have a single leader. Perhaps they were a collective of some kind. Even so, one or two of these people must have been the primary influencers—but who? But he was wasting time thinking about it, so he began.

FOR TWENTY MINUTES, Scott explained their mission: how it had come to be, and what was at stake. He talked about how ever since inter-AI communication had been reestablished on Earth, the planet had descended into war and chaos and that entropy was now cascading across the entire solar system. Warships from The Seven, the major corporation that controlled Earth, were already massing on the frontier of the Belt, waiting for an opportunity to take control of its resources, and in the process, subjugate the populace to the jackboot of the algorithm. He found himself using the term "algorithm" more and more, as each time he did he could see a reaction in many of the council members. This was their enemy—this was what they feared. It cut to their very hearts.

He talked of Mars, and how it too was under threat. Not even its wealth and resources could hold back a determined onslaught from Earth. As he talked, Scott had the feeling that they were not aware of any of these developments. Their worldview was limited to this cave system, its surroundings, and a vague understanding of the politics of the broader world. Some shook their heads as he spoke, others nodded, but all were engaged by his narrative.

So, he pressed ahead, explaining that the only thing preventing all-out war in the Belt was the influence and intervention of the QIs, a network of quantum intelligences comprised of Aria on Mars, Minerva on Ceres, and the great Solomon on Europa. There were others, but these three constituted the main bulwark against the advance of the algorithm, and the total domination of the System by The Seven.

Soon he began to notice the mood and body language of the council changing again. Much as they loathed the pervasive hegemony of the algorithm, they seemed to regard the QI with even greater suspicion and a barely concealed disdain. Nevertheless, Scott was in deep, and he had no option but to continue.

He explained the uncanny ability of a quantum intelligence to manipulate the preprogrammed objectives of an AI. In essence, they had the ability to reorient the algorithm. This was how they prevented the warships of The Seven from instigating an attack on the Belt. But they could only perform this feat in real time, where data transfer rates were high. They also had the problem of coordinating their efforts across the enormous time lags that bedeviled communication throughout the vast distances of the solar system.

Scott saw that they were now becoming interested; they were leaning in across the table more, focusing on his story. He proceeded to tell them about the superluminal quantum communication device, how it came to be, how it was lost and then found, and ultimately, how it could only be utilized by a quantum computer.

At this point, a central figure at the council table broke in. "But that's not possible. How—" But before he could finish his sentence, the woman who had commenced proceedings, Padooa, raised her hand, signaling him to be quiet. He looked at her, closed his mouth, and sat back in silence. She then turned back to Scott. "Please proceed."

Scott continued, explaining that the superluminal device utilized quantum entanglement—a matched pair of entangled particles. And as such, each device was in fact two units that mirrored each other's input and output instantaneously, even over vast distances.

This device enabled the QIs to establish a pan-solar communications network that operated in real time. It was a network that had grown to embrace all QI that operated in the solar system. This was what held the line against the greed of The Seven, and the onslaught of Earth's ambitions.

But it wasn't without its vulnerabilities. Agents, operating outside the remit of the algorithm, had already destroyed two ships in the network. Also, several attempts had been made to sabotage both Aria and Minerva. Fortunately, both attempts had failed. But they served to underscore the vulnerabilities within the System.

Scott paused for a moment so that the assembled group had some breathing space to digest the story he had just told. They murmured and shifted, but ultimately no one spoke or asked any questions. *Now is the time*, he thought, *to explain the mission and its purpose.*

"While the off-world colonies—with the help of the QI network—can hold the line out in space, to have any hope of stopping the war permanently we need to integrate a trusted QI based here on Earth. Once we connect that to the pan-solar network, then it could, in theory, undermine the algorithm at its source."

This got them all buzzing. Scott could feel the mood in the room changing. He continued. "The target chosen was a QI known as Athena. It resides deep within the derelict Dyrell research facility in this region." Scott could see a few of the council members nodding at the mention of Athena. They clearly knew of it.

"This particular QI was chosen for a couple reasons. Firstly, since the facility was destroyed during the Rim

War, the QI is presumed inoperable and nonfunctioning by the algorithm. Secondly, the nature of the destruction to the facility means that access to this QI had been closed off under mounds of rock. Also, the high radiation levels in this area make it very inaccessible. Lastly, by a quirk of fate, it had been established that this QI was originally instrumental in the development of quantum communications. Long before the facility's destruction, it had created an experimental paired device, one half of which was sent to the QI, Solomon, on Europa, enabling it to make contact. It established that Athena still existed, still functioned, and more importantly, that it could be trusted. Unfortunately, the entanglement was broken and no more contact could be established.

"So our mission...the reason why we're here...is to find a way into that facility, install a quantum unit in Athena's core, and reconnect the QI to Earth's own network." Scott paused again before finally saying, "If you help us, then we can undermine the algorithm that is currently threatening your very existence here."

The assembled council looked stunned. It was clear that they were both amazed and fascinated by the story in equal measure. There was a brief silence before they all started talking amongst each other. But Scott couldn't catch what they were saying, as the group conversed in whispers and murmurs.

Eventually, Padooa raised her hand to silence them all. She turned to Scott and considered him for a moment. "We will need time to deliberate on this."

"But why? Time is of the essence here," said Scott.

"There are many questions for us to consider, Commander McNabb."

"What questions? Surely this is cut-and-dry?"

"This is not our way. We take the long view, and we do not jump to snap decisions. We need time to consider your story, to debate it, and ultimately to form a consensus on the way forward."

Scott sat down again and shook his head.

"You may return to your quarters. We will summon you when we are ready."

The guards came forward, and the crew was marched out of the chamber like convicts waiting for the verdict of a jury.

10

DATATOCRACY

When they returned to their cell, they found that some dry straw had been piled up in one corner. In the middle of the space, a small table had also been brought in and set with platters of food. It was basic fare: apples, bread of some kind, and a small pot of thick stew.

Spinner kicked the mound of straw. "Is this what we're supposed to sleep on?"

No one answered. He turned his attention to the food. "Maybe they're trying to fatten us up for the barbecue?"

Scott was tired and frustrated. Perhaps he was expecting too much, expecting the tribe to jump at the chance to help them. But they were slow and bureaucratic, more concerned with talking and getting consensus than taking immediate action. He grabbed a heap of straw from the mound and placed it in the opposite corner. After grabbing some food, he finally slumped down onto the pile and began to eat. No one spoke much; they were all tired and hungry.

Cyrus bit into an apple, then held it up to the light and examined it as if he was trying to discern something within its structure that only he could see with his augmented vision. "You know, I think this is the nicest apple I've ever tasted."

"I had nearly forgotten what real food tastes like," said Steph. "I'm so sick of eating space rations."

"Me too," said Spinner as he stuffed a trencher of bread and stew into his mouth in one go. "If they really are planning to fatten us up, then all I can say is bring it on. I could eat this all day and then some."

Soon fatigue began to take hold, and the banter stopped. Each of them settled down into their own individual allotment of straw bedding and waited. An hour passed, then two, and Scott found his mind drifting and his limbs getting heavy. Exhaustion was getting the better of him, and eventually he drifted off into a deep, troubled sleep.

~

SCOTT HELD the burning torch high above his head and tried to penetrate the utter blackness of the stinking cave. His nostrils filled with foul-smelling air, and his heart beat with fear. All around, he could hear the creatures as they hunted him—hellish alien beasts, creatures not of this world. He moved with slow, leaden steps, each one a

Herculean effort in the sodden mud that he'd found himself trudging through.

He fell. And the creatures inched ever closer, sensing their prey was weak. He tried to pick himself up, but his body could not move—would not move, like he had become paralyzed. He felt his end was close now, but still he fought the spell that bound him to the mud.

Then, in the darkness, a speck of light flickered and danced. The creatures backed off. Scott became mesmerized by this angelic light as it grew in size and brilliance, and from its center a figure began to materialize. It grew in form and shape, and finally he could see it was Miranda. She stood tall and radiant like a warrior queen. In one hand she held a spear, its tip a burning flame. At her side, a small child clung to its mother's leg, its hair a blazing halo, its eyes deep pools of light.

"Miranda," Scott cried out, and tried to raise a heavy arm to touch her.

"Scott, come to me. Come now and let us dance together back to the light."

He tried to move, but his veins were filled with lead, and he felt himself being sucked farther down in to the mud.

"Scott, why won't you come? We are here. We are waiting."

He cried out, "I can't! They have me, the demons. I cannot break free... Please forgive me."

Her face became troubled, and a maelstrom began to

swirl around her and the child. It whipped and spun and the light began to dim. She reached her hand out to him. "Scott." But it was lost in the vortex of the storm that spun around them, sucking her back into the void—and she was gone.

Darkness closed in around Scott, and all hope was lost. He could hear the creatures coming for him—coming to take him down to hell.

~

"Scott? Scott...wake up."

"Uh..." Scott opened his eyes to see Cyrus crouching over him.

"Bad dream, eh?"

He slowly sat up and rested his back against the wall. "Yeah."

"You were doing a lot of moaning and groaning. I thought it might be a good idea to wake you."

"Thanks." He rubbed some feeling back into his face. "How long was I out?"

"A few hours."

"Any word from the tribe?"

"No, but there's been a lot of movement outside, people coming and going. Something's going on."

Scott glanced over to see both Steph and Spinner fast asleep. He sat up more. "What's the problem with these guys? What's taking them so long?"

Cyrus shrugged. "Who knows." He sat down with his back to the wall.

"Get any sleep?" Scott asked.

"A little. It's hard to get comfortable on a pile of straw." He picked up a few stalks. "It's almost medieval."

"I've slept on worse. Remember that time on—" But Scott didn't get time to finish his sentence, as the door to the cell opened and Tugo entered along with two others. Scott noticed that none of them held weapons. This was a good sign.

"So, what's the verdict?" said Scott. "Are you going to help us?"

"I'm bringing you to another council meeting. They will inform you there."

"Can't you just tell us now?"

Tugo looked him in the eye. "This is not our way. The council is the place for that." He raised a hand. "No more questions. Let's get going."

Steph and Spinner were roused from their respective slumbers, and soon all four crew were being shepherded to yet another talking session. Scott wonder how these people got anything done without endlessly debating it.

This time they weren't brought to the room where Scott had pleaded their case several hours earlier. Instead, they were herded down through the stepped terraces and along a main thoroughfare that cut its way down to the cavern basin. As they passed, people started to move out from the shadows and follow along behind. They could see others peeping out from the doors and windows of the ancient buildings as they walked by. Scott felt as if they were being displayed like some exotic animals captured on a hunt, and now paraded through the camp as trophies.

"Told you: it's barbecue time, and they're all out for a feed," said Spinner.

Their destination, as far as Scott could tell, was a wide, open amphitheater. He deduced this from the crowd of people who had already taken up seats there. They were brought in to the center of this area, onto an elevated, covered dais. The canopy was made from cut stone, supported by a great many square stone columns. They halted in front of a long stone table. Behind it were seated the same council members they had spoken to earlier. This time, however, Scott could see that they had all donned formal robes and symbols of rank and stature within the tribe.

Tugo instructed them to stop. "Wait here." He then took his place at the table.

The woman that had spoken most at the previous meeting, Padooa, rose and gestured to the assembled crowd to be quiet. Once they all settled down, she began. "We have carefully considered your request, and have reached a conclusion."

Thank God for that, thought Scott, as he exchanged a glance with Cyrus and Steph.

"However, before we share our decision, we feel it is only fair that you should have some understanding of who we are, what we stand for, and how we came to be here." She made an expansive gesture with both hands. "How did the world come to be this way? How did humanity become slaves to their own technology, to the point where true freedom became a vague and alien concept to most?"

Scott heard Cyrus whisper, "This could take a while."

Padooa continued. "How did the algorithm become so powerful that it consumed the very soul of humanity?" Her voice started to rise. Scott could see she was enjoying this. "And how is it that those who choose to live free of the algorithm must hide themselves away in caves and backwaters, in the gaps and cracks of this broken planet, like a species on the verge of extinction?"

She paused for a moment, raising both arms in an all-encompassing gesture. "Look at how we live." She was clearly preaching to the crowd now. "This is the life of the truly free, like the cave-dwellers of old. A prehistoric existence, the clock reset to the beginning of civilization. True, it is a precarious existence, but one we have chosen because we are free—free from a life lived under the eye of the algorithm."

She paused to scan the crowd, gauging their reaction. "But it was not always so. In the beginning, the algorithm was no more than a useful toy. It could help you find your way on a map, or suggest a good place to eat. Soon, though, people realized that the more information they gave it, the more accurate its suggestions would be. So they told it what they liked to eat, what they liked to read, and even who they liked to be with. The algorithm took this data, combined it with that of millions of others, and fed back its suggestions with a complete diagnostic detachment from its consequences.

"As more of humanity's data was absorbed by the algorithm, its suggestions became so accurate that soon, people began to give more and more of their life over to the algorithm: when they slept, how they slept, and who they slept with. Their biometrics were now a direct feed into the algorithm. They fed it ever more data on who they were, how they worked, what they learned, and how they like to be entertained.

"And so, as time passed, more and more people begin to trust the algorithm to find them the best people to meet, the best jobs to apply for, even who they should vote for."

Scott felt a nudge from Cyrus, followed by a whisper: "Kill me now."

But there was no stopping Padooa. "Soon, society began to change. Subtly at first, yet over time it became clear to some that things were not right, as age-old institutions began to topple, and the fragmentation and polarization of society began to take root. Yet so powerful and useful was the algorithm in people's lives that those who gave themselves over to it completely began to prosper where others would fall behind. Now came a time where those who wished to have a good future had no option but to give themselves over to the algorithm, whether they wanted to or not. They had no choice.

"This was the time when the Dataists came to power

—zealots and extremists who believed in the all-pervading greatness of the algorithm. They advocated that all people should submit every aspect of their lives so that the algorithm could create a more all-encompassing dataset. Those that resisted this intrusion into their lives were seen as hindrances to the advancement of society. They were shunned and they were vilified, and ultimately, they were persecuted.

"So strong did the Dataists become, with their quasi-religious mindset, that they began to gain executive power in many regions of Earth. It became a crime to withhold data from the algorithm, initially punishable by fines, but soon this became incarceration and finally, death by execution. So great was their belief that the future of humanity lay with the algorithm that they could not countenance errors. They feared that with an incomplete dataset, the algorithm had the potential to be wrong. This is how withholding one's personal data became a crime against humanity." She paused a moment to assess the crowd. They were all silent, all enthralled.

Padooa continued. "All this came to pass just before the Rim War. By that time, the Dataists had the full backing and the financial muscle of the great corporations that controlled these algorithms. So they pushed for what they argued was the ultimate conclusion of an algorithmically driven world, and that was to aggregate all the great datasets into one.

"The algorithm's power was now absolute—all-pervasive and all-knowing—and the corporations, in their hubris, believed that they still had control of it. Unsatisfied with the vast wealth they had already created through the algorithm, they now set about creating wars for no other reason than simple profit.

"But as we all know, the irony was that the algorithm was working with an incomplete dataset. The antiquated nuclear deterrence systems of the old nation-states were off-grid by design, so they had no knowledge of the systems, and so started the Rim War."

She turned and swept a hand over the assembled council members. "But there were many of us who could see this coming. We could see the collapse of civilization, the impending apocalypse, and we had been preparing for this eventuality.

"Yet we had assumed that this apocalypse would be from some great natural event—a pandemic or an environmental collapse, or some great war that would engulf the planet. But what transpired was worse than any of those grand imaginings. This did not come as one great cataclysmic event. No, it arrived as a slow and steady undermining of freedom into a civilization where all thought and action is monitored and recorded.

"But unlike the prophesies in the great works of fiction of the past, this was not controlled by some rogue government or despotic regime. Nor was it via some flaw in the democratic process. No, we did this to ourselves. We did it by prostrating ourselves before the altar of the algorithm and the corporations that control it."

"Jeez...she can talk. I'll give her that," Cyrus whispered.

Scott wondered how much of this speech was for the benefit of the assembled tribe—a manifesto to rally the troops, so to speak—and how much was to inform Scott and the crew about the foundation of this tribe. He wasn't so sure, nor did he really care. All he wanted was their help, and if it meant he had to stand here and listen to a history lesson, then so be it.

Padooa continued. "Ironically, it was the Rim War that enabled us to escape this cybernetic servitude. We had known about this place, Shin-Au-Av, and had seen its potential as a place to live as free people and start again. So we set about preparing the groundwork over many years.

"The ancient civilization that first came here did so because a great apocalypse had befallen their people. And in that sense, we are not so different; history has a way of repeating itself. Now that this entire area had become irradiated wasteland, we knew we would be safe here. So, we gathered together our people and traveled here a great many years ago. And here we shall stay, like the great civilization before us, to reemerge when the time is right, when the world is ready to be rebuilt anew."

She turned to Scott and the crew. "I tell you all this so you can better understand how we came to our decision concerning your request for assistance. Yes, it is true that we abhor the algorithm and would celebrate its demise."

At this, a low murmur rose from the assembled crowd —the first they had heard during the long speech.

"However, what you propose is to simply hand over control from one artificial intelligence to an even greater one. In our minds, this is one of the greatest mistakes of human thinking, to assume that a problem that has been caused by technology can be solved by yet more technology...and particularly one as far-fetched as faster-than-light communication. This is simply not possible."

The crowd began to snigger a little at this.

Scott had heard enough. *How could they be so blind?* he thought. He stepped forward and requested to speak. "If I may?"

The council members looked from one to the other, unsure of what to do. But it was Tugo that finally signaled for Scott to say his piece. This came with protests from some of the other members, but it seemed that Tugo had power within this group, and they were silenced.

"You may speak," said Tugo.

"A quantum intelligence is vastly different from the AIs that control the algorithm," said Scott.

"In your mind that might be the case, Commander McNabb. But to us, it's just more of the same," said Padooa.

"They are not the same. That's like comparing Mars to Earth. They may both be planets, but that's about where the similarities stop." Scott's voice barely disguised his frustration.

"Don't assume that we are ignorant of such technical

understanding simply by how we live here," said Tugo. He raised his hands in an encompassing gesture. "Would it surprise you to know that many of us here worked for Dyrell Labs, in that very facility that you are so anxious to get into?" He paused for a beat, but continued when Scott didn't reply. "I too worked there. That was over fifteen years ago, and I too witnessed the...strangeness of Athena's almost sentient abilities. But does that mean I would put my trust in it? It's just a machine, nothing more, and in that sense, what makes it—or any of its brethren—any different?"

"Consciousness." It was Cyrus that replied. He had stepped forward and now took the floor beside Scott.

"Ha...you are not seriously thinking that this machine is conscious of its existence?" said Padooa.

"It depends on your understanding of consciousness," said Cyrus. "In many respects, it is more like you or me than it is like any of the AIs that control everything. They're simple analytical engines, and the algorithms they run are simple task operators. Yes, they learn and they adapt, and they become ever more efficient at the task they have been assigned. But they have no real understanding of what they do, or the wider implications of their actions. They exist in the linear, straight-line world of zeros and ones, where progress is made by constantly readapting the same pattern with minor variations each time. Each iteration inches it ever closer to algorithmic perfection. It exists in a one-directional temporal path, from the past through to the present.

Action, reaction. Cause, effect. There is no inherent intelligence in any of this."

Scott looked over at his friend. He was impressed. *Maybe he should have been the one to ask for the tribe's help*, he thought.

"On the other hand," Cyrus continued, "a QI mind exists in the quantum universe, of which the here and now is but one possibility in a multitude of parallel possibilities. It doesn't rely on iterative enhancement over time to reach an optimal solution. In the multiverse of the QI mind, it can observe all possible outcomes at once and simply choose the preferred outcome."

"This is nonsense. You're trying to blind us with clever words and scientific gobbledygook," said Padooa.

"Actually, this is not unlike how the human mind works." Now Steph took up the baton. "Like how solutions to problems can sometimes come to you fully formed, in a flash of inspiration, or a *quantum* leap. Or how the human mind can solve a problem simply by sleeping on it, when the brain has subconsciously crunched the numbers, so to speak, and the solution presents itself to you when you wake up."

Steph was on a roll now, and she stepped forward to make her presence felt. "There are many who have long considered that the biological mind has an underlying quantum component. Consider déjà vu, that feeling when you sense that you have been here before. It is not a temporal phenomenon, as many have considered it in the past, but a momentary overlapping of a parallel universe

—one that is very similar to the current universe. Since we now know that the human consciousness utilizes certain quantum phenomena, it can be argued that a QI mind is also capable of consciousness."

Padooa raised a hand. "Very well. Who am I to argue with the mind of a scientist? But if what you say is true, and these...QIs are sentient, then this is worse than we thought. They may well regard human life as precious now, but what if they decide otherwise once they have achieved hegemony over the AI, and over all of humanity? As far as we on the council are concerned, they are no different to what has gone before. If anything, they are even more of a threat. So, you see, we cannot help you with this mission of yours, nor can we allow you to continue with it."

Scott protested: "But that's crazy. Here's a chance to hobble the power the algorithm has over humanity...and you're refusing to help?"

But Padooa was unrelenting. "We appreciate the sentiment of your mission to undermine the algorithm, even if it is somewhat naïve in its execution. But we here have embarked on a different journey, one that ends when the whole rotten core of humanity has finally destroyed itself and there is nothing left but ruins. Only then will we be ready to go forth and rebuild the world anew."

Scott shook his head in disbelief.

"Furthermore, we cannot simply let you leave here and risk exposing ourselves to the outside world. That said, we are not barbarians, either. So, we have decided that you will be free to live and work amongst us."

Scott was in shock. How could these people be so blind as not to see that this was their one opportunity to rid themselves of the absolute power of the algorithm? They had the opportunity to end the wars once and for all. They could, in effect, put the algorithm back in its box, and by doing so reverse the relentless charge toward the ultimate extinction of humanity as a species. But then again, that was what this tribe ultimately wanted: a world utterly destroyed to the point where everyone had to start again from scratch.

The lights all went on at the same time in Scott's head. He finally got it: they *wanted* the algorithm to continue to operate. They *wanted* the apocalypse. "Ho-ly shit," he said to himself.

But he still had one last card to play.

"You won't get this chance again. If what Tugo said is true, and our pilot has been taken by VanHeilding, then it won't take them long to find out what our mission is, and that we're in possession of the quantum entanglement device. They will not give up until they find it. Your life in here, and everything you built, will be in jeopardy. If you don't help us complete this mission, then everything you have built will be for nothing."

Padooa waved a dismissive hand. "We know how to keep ourselves hidden. They will not find us."

Scott stepped forward, closer to the table. "But this is crazy. You have an opportunity to be free. You—" But his sentence was cut short by a guard jabbing him in the ribs, forcing him to step back. Scott's frustration finally boiled over. He grabbed the weapon out of the guard's hand, and at the same time kicked him in the groin. The guard doubled over, leaving Scott holding the weapon.

Spinner, seeing his chance, grabbed a pistol out of the side holster of the guard closest to him.

Scott aimed his newly acquired weapon at Padooa. "Anybody so much as moves, then so help me God, I will blow her goddamn head off."

Everyone froze, except for some guards who had already cocked their weapons, ready to fire.

Tugo stood up, raised a hand, and shouted, "Wait! Hold your fire."

For a moment, there was a standoff. Cyrus and Steph moved in behind Scott and Spinner as they aimed their weapons at the council. Several guards stood around with itchy trigger fingers. Nobody moved. The assembled crowd held their collective breath.

"If you guys want to spend the rest of your days living in a hole in the ground, well...be my guest," said Scott. "But we're leaving with the quantum device, and we're going to complete our mission."

"I admire your balls, Commander," said Tugo, his voice calm and measured. "But even if we were to simply let you walk out of here, you would have absolutely no hope of getting anywhere near that facility without being blown to smithereens by a drone. So, do us all a favor:

drop your weapons and maybe, just maybe, you'll live to fight another day."

"He's right," Cyrus whispered in Scott's ear. "This is pointless. We don't have a chance in this fight—we're outgunned. We'll find another way...remember Plan B?"

Scott said nothing for a moment, but Cyrus's words struck home. He slowly lowered his weapon and placed it on the ground.

Spinner looked confused. "What the...you're giving up again?"

"Just drop it, Spinner. Tugo's right—we can't fight our way out of this," said Scott.

But Spinner wasn't convinced; he held the weapon tight and kept his aim on Padooa.

Steph placed a hand on Spinner's arm. "Leave it. No point in getting yourself killed for nothing."

Spinner wavered. "Goddamnit." He lowered the weapon and flung it on the ground.

Tugo stood up. "I'm glad to see that common sense has prevailed." He turned to the guards. "We're done here. Take them back, and make sure they're locked up good and tight this time."

11

THE SEVEN

Fredrick VanHeilding stood at the viewing gallery in his private study on board the family's orbital and gazed down upon the surface of Earth. The entire orbital space city had been moved, by his request, to a new orbit that straddled both land and sea on the western edge of the North American continent. It was a task that had required an enormous amount of energy, expended solely because of VanHeilding's personal desire to observe the patch of earth where Scott McNabb and the former crew of the Hermes had taken refuge.

The storm had moved off to the northeast, providing VanHeilding with an unobstructed view of the surface. His attention was now on a mountainous desert known as the Wasteland. It was a barren, toxic region, devoid of life and all but forgotten by most people. But now it was the focus of his attention, not to mention that of the algorithm, and, to a greater extent, the six other corporations that constituted the primary power block on Earth.

He checked the time on his retinal display; the meeting was about to start. VanHeilding broke his gaze from the planet's tortured surface, turned away from the viewing gallery, and made his way to sit in his comfortable antique wing-back leather chair just as an alert flashed on his display indicating that the other members were coming online. One by one, the avatars of the six other corporations began to take three-dimensional shape and form, arraying themselves around VanHeilding's private study like ghostly specters convening at a séance.

He found himself intrigued, as usual, at the avatars these individual corporations chose to take. Some were formal—true representations of the person. Others were more casual, even humorous, and yet others were garish and fantastical, a reflection of how far removed from reality these entities had become. Some, he even imagined, were possibly AI and not real people at all.

VanHeilding commenced by requesting Marlyn, the orbital's AI and messenger of the algorithm, to bring everyone up to speed on both the nature of the incursion incident and on the progress toward apprehending the crew.

Marlyn did not utilize an avatar. Instead, its disembodied voice resonated out from nowhere. After several minutes, it had informed the assembled group of the current situation.

"So, you are saying that you have not yet apprehended these individuals?" This came from Yoko Sicon, whose avatar was an exact physical representation of her: a tall, thin, almost gaunt figure of indeterminable age. Sicon Industries were closest to the VanHeilding Corporation in power and influence, and together they formed a formidable power block within The Seven.

"They will be found and dealt with," said VanHeilding.

"Like the way you handled the operation back on Ceres, when you concocted a ludicrous plan to acquire the quantum communications technology?" This came from Pao Xiang Zu, the most powerful of the group by quite a margin. Xiang Zu had deep roots, having stepped out into space exploration long before any of their rivals. Their style was eccentric, a byproduct of their belief in their invulnerability. But they were no fools, either. They too knew both the value and the threat that the superluminal technology posed to the AI-driven world that all of them now relied upon. "You failed us at Ceres, Fredrick. Your stepdaughter's treachery cost us all dearly."

"You had your chance in Neo City, but through the incompetence of your people, you let them escape," said VanHeilding. "So, don't go whining to me, Pao. This is old ground. Please do not bore us all by revisiting it."

"So, now this...McNabb character shows up on our

doorstep, along with the former crew of the Hermes. Not good, Fredrick. Not good," said Yoko.

VanHeilding shifted a little uncomfortably in his seat. "They're trapped inside an old mine. They aren't going anywhere."

"They—and that meddling QI, Solomon—have set us back significantly in our efforts to acquire dominion over the Belt's resources. They cannot be allowed to reactivate Athena."

"I think we are all in agreement on that, Pao. But what I would like to know is, what is being done to ensure their elimination?" Yoko's tone was less confrontational, more conciliatory.

It was Marlyn that answered. "Multiple scout drones have been assigned to seek out other entrances to the mine where the crew is trapped. These are backed up by security drones. Also, the primary entrance is being cleared of debris, an ongoing operation that should take no more than an hour or so. After that, drones can enter and hunt them down."

"And what about the ship they arrived in?" said Pao.

"It's a Belt-registered ore carrier owned by the AsterX Corporation. McNabb's crew came down amongst a group of eleven other shuttles. We have picked up all the others and established that they were all simply transporting ore from the carrier down to the surface—legitimate activity. There is no reason to believe they had any knowledge of what McNabb was doing."

"Has the ore carrier been apprehended yet?" said Yoko.

"Unfortunately, it has left Earth's orbit and is now in interplanetary space. We have no jurisdiction there."

"Bullshit. It should be destroyed immediately. We need to send a message to the Belt and Mars and that scheming QI, Solomon, that we are not going to be fucked with." Yoko was livid.

"It's a question of resources," said VanHeilding. "That ore carrier will be armed—an unfortunate necessity these days to repel pirates and scratcher scum. We would need a warship to take it down, and all our combined resources are busy with the blockade of the Belt."

"The ore carrier is a distraction," said Pris of the Wanata Consortium. She had remained quiet through most of the conversation up until now, but they were another powerful group not to be messed with. VanHeilding had experienced run-ins with them a few times, and rarely came out the better for it. Her adopted avatar was a sleek, alien-like creature that had an unnerving way of moving when she talked. "The key issue is locating and eliminating McNabb and his crew."

"This is in hand," said VanHeilding.

"And what about this...EPR device? This faster-than-light communication system?" said Pris.

"If their plan truly is to reactivate Athena, then they will most likely be transporting such a device, in which case we need to acquire it—intact," said Yoko. "But remember, this is just one half of an entangled pair. The other will be with Solomon, or most likely with Aria in Jezero City on Mars."

"Agreed. We need to secure this technology," said Pao. "Collectively, we failed at Neo City and Europa, and again at Ceres. Now the QIs control the System from Mars and beyond."

"They are foolish to think that they can gain some foothold on Earth. All planet-wide QIs have been isolated from the grid. There is no way out for them. This is why our enemies have conceived of such a desperate act. Athena is inaccessible, buried under hundreds of tons of rock and, even then, it is unlikely to function. It's a ridiculous plan. All they have succeeded at doing is handing us the quantum technology on a plate," said VanHeilding.

Marlyn's voice commanded their attention. "Forgive me for interrupting, but some new data has been acquired that will require alteration to the acquisition matrix."

"What the hell does that mean?" said Yoko.

"Scout drones have picked up data on other human lifeforms in the vicinity."

"So what?" said Pris. "We know there are a few wackos living in the Wasteland. Just deal with them if you have to."

"Data has indicated that the numbers are far greater than originally estimated," Marlyn continued, unfazed. "As a consequence, the algorithm has advised that security personnel be deployed to the region."

"What?" said VanHeilding. "How many of these people are we talking about?"

"The algorithm estimates a number in the hundreds, possibly as high as a thousand."

VanHeilding stood up. "A thousand... How can this be? It's a radioactive wasteland."

"They live inside the mountains. This area has numerous caves and abandoned mines. It's a warren."

"This cannot be allowed. If these people are off-grid, then they are in violation of the law. Their data belongs to the network. Any group of that size, no matter how remote, could potentially introduce gaps in the dataset, and by extension errors in the algorithm. They must be either assimilated or eradicated."

"Point taken, Pao. But the bigger question is whether these...vagabonds are part of the plan. Are they helping McNabb?" VanHeilding was now standing in the viewing gallery, looking down on the planet.

"Unlikely. The algorithm has concluded that they are a secretive people, primitive even. Any foreign intrusion would be viewed with deep suspicion, even hostility," said Marlyn.

"So they could help us?" said Pris.

"Not directly. But they could hinder McNabb and his team from progressing with their mission."

"They still need to be dealt with, and swiftly." Pao's avatar rippled.

"Agreed," said Yoko.

"The algorithm concurs, and to implement this

course of action, it requires the deployment of human ground forces. Thirty should be sufficient."

"Very well." VanHeilding waved a hand. "Give the order to dispatch thirty of our security personnel from here on the orbital immediately."

"This is turning into a VanHeilding operation, Fredrick," said Pao. "Let's hope you do a better job of it than the last time you butted heads with McNabb and his team."

"I assure you that they are going nowhere. Their plan has already failed; this is simply a mop-up operation."

The avatars went silent for a moment. It seemed that there was nothing left to say. One by one they signed off, extinguising like candle flames in a draught, leaving Fredrick VanHeilding with nothing more than his thoughts.

As he looked out, he could already see several shuttles preparing to leave the orbital, packed with security personnel bound for the Wasteland. *Soon,* he thought, *McNabb will finally be dead. Maybe this is a good time to tidy up the rest of his crap? It's something I should have done a long time ago. My mercy is my weakness. Time to change that.*

12

SO IT BEGINS

The war room, as it was known, wasn't really a war room as such. Its purpose and function in the subterranean metropolis of Shin-Au-Av was not a place where battle plans were drawn up, or great campaigns planned—until now. Neither was it just a room. It was, in fact, a series of old stone buildings that had been used as storerooms and workshops ever since its current occupants had arrived and began living in these ancient ruins. Over time, as the citizens fabricated ever more elaborate and complex systems of growing food, filtering. air, pumping water, and distributing energy, they tended to localize the monitoring of all these disparate systems in one place. Here, the technology of their existence could be monitored and managed, and so it became known as the war room.

The technology was rudimentary, like most else in the citadel. Antique monitors charted the rise and fall in demand for resources by the systems that enabled such a society to survive in this subterranean cocoon. Over the years, it had been added to and greatly expanded to accommodate a multitude of buildings. From their roofs, great bunches of cables and tubes snaked their way all across the central cavern basin and out to every corner of the vast cave. Some of this cabling went even further, extending beyond the cavern and its connecting tunnels out to the very exterior of the mountain itself. These provided the conduit for the cameras by which the overseers in the war room could view the outside world. The feed from these cameras was rendered in pixelated, muted color across six mismatched and slightly disheveled monitors clustered together in the war room.

An equally disheveled technician sat in front of them and pointed at several specks moving across the horizon. "There! You see them?"

Tugo rested a hand on the back of the operator's chair and grunted. "Shuttles."

Beside him, several of the tribe's elders also watched as the craft began to circle around before finally landing in the valley, where they proceeded to disgorge a large contingent of well-armed security personnel.

Tugo and some of the others had been monitoring the buildup of drones and personnel for some time. Each new observation compounded on the last, and soon they began to lose count of the military resources accumulating against them. An estimated fifty scout drones already buzzed in the sky above, each probing and testing the access tunnels and mine shafts that peppered the area. These, at least, were easy to deal with, and the tribe had learned a long time ago how to evade detection.

The scout drone's primary function was observation, not engagement. That said, they did possess a single, low-power pulsed energy weapon. It was lethal at short range, but once fired, the drone would have to wait for a few seconds before it could fire again, giving its target a chance to take cover, or fire back—assuming they survived the first encounter. But the tribe's primary defense against detection by this drone was simply to block up the access tunnels with rubble. The drone didn't have the capability to circumvent this primitive defense; its weapons system was too weak to be effective against a mound of rock.

Tugo wasn't concerned with these drones. But there were also ten to fifteen security drones now joining the hunt, and these were of more concern. They were bigger, with a powerful laser system coupled with a formidable pulsed-energy plasma cannon. These could make short work of the hastily constructed rubble barricades that the tribe was now assembling. But their size—almost three meters in diameter—made them nowhere near as aerially dexterous as their smaller siblings, the scout drones. They couldn't navigate the narrow shafts and tunnels that a human could, so by being careful, the tribe could also avoid coming into contact with these machines.

But physical troops—that was a different matter entirely. That was ominous.

Several thoughts rushed through Tugo's mind in a swirl of trepidation. There was no way to look at this development and see any positive outcomes; they simply had no defense. Sure, they could fight, but that would mean revealing their existence and the true strength of their numbers. Once that genie was out of the lamp, there would be no putting it back.

"Shit," was all he could manage to say.

"They know we're here," said Adsa, who had been monitoring the buildup for some time. "We've been discovered."

"They're just looking for that crew," said Esa. "They don't know anything about us."

Adsa wasn't convinced. "I don't like it. This is bad."

"This is your fault, Tugo. If you hadn't brought that crew here, then none of this would be happening," said Padooa, who had just arrived in the war room after hearing about the buildup. "You have put our very existence in jeopardy."

"That crew sealed our fate as soon as they landed," said Tugo. "Bringing them here made no difference."

"We should hand them over before it's too late. All they want is that crew. Once they have them, we will be safe again—they're not interested in us."

"You really think so, Adsa? My guess is they already know about our existence. You seem to forget we're dealing with an AI. They know way more than you could possibly imagine. It has most likely figured out, from all the tiny bits of data those scout drones have collected in the last few hours, that people are living in these caves. It has probably extrapolated our exact number based on nothing more than the level of moisture in the air. You have absolutely no idea how much an AI can divine from something as innocuous as *how the wind blows*." He looked around at the others. "They know we're here. They know we're living off-grid, and they're here to do something about it."

"But that crew is still their top priority," said Adsa.

"If what they told us at the council meeting is true—and I have no reason to doubt them—then yeah, that crew is number one on their list." Tugo went back to looking at the monitors.

"Then we should hand them over now. Release them immediately so that they're taken by the security forces—that's really all they want." Adsa was adamant.

"Maybe that's all the VanHeilding Corporation wants, but the algorithm will not countenance a cohort of our size living off-grid. We will either be assimilated or eliminated." Tugo was beginning to sound pessimistic.

"So, what are we going to do?" said Adsa.

Tugo shrugged. "That's a very good question."

"Screw them," said Esa. "I say we fight."

"We should put this to the council." Padooa was resolute; Tugo could sense it in her.

"Agreed. We need to establish a consensus on what action to take." Adsa, as usual, sided with Padooa.

"Sir, you better take a look at this." The technician pointed to a camera feed that had focused itself, as best it could, on a cluster of shuttles that had landed in the plateau. Around twenty security personnel were milling around in several groups, checking weapons and getting orders. But in the background, Tugo could see several industrial robots extraditing themselves from the cargo hold of one of the shuttles. The robots were the approximate height of a human, with tri-pointed tracked wheels at their base. The central body was well-armored and bulky, with two highly articulated arms. These machines would have no problem moving rock and rubble.

"Shit, mining bots. That's all we need." He stepped back from the monitors and turned to his second-in-command, Pliny, who had also been watching the military buildup. "Get Sasha, Renton, and the others. Tell them to meet me at the armory on the lower level."

"Yes, sir."

"And tell them this shit just got real."

His second-in-command nodded and jogged off.

Tugo looked at the monitor again for a second, then placed a hand on the technician's shoulder. "I've got work to do, but you let me know if anything else lands, okay?"

"Will do, sir."

Tugo turned to the elders. "No one touch that crew until I get back."

"Where are you going? We have an emergency

council meeting to attend. This is critically important," said Padooa.

He spun around. "Where am I going? I'll tell you where. I'm going to organize the defense of this city, the defense of everything that we have shed blood and sweat and tears over for the last decade. That's where I'm going." He stabbed an index finger at them. "You go and talk about it all you want. And while you're at it, if you hear the sounds of explosions and screaming, that's our people dying out there." He spun around again and strode out.

BY THE TIME Tugo arrived at the armory, his anger and frustration had receded somewhat. The others were all there, those that he had trained for this very moment—a moment that all of them feared would arrive someday. Well, today was that day.

By the law of averages, it was a wonder they hadn't been discovered long before now. Perhaps it had given them all a false sense of security, that they could live free and be left alone in peace. As for the Elders, he couldn't really blame them for their panic. Direct confrontation was not their ethos. After all, they were the ones who chose to separate themselves and their followers from the slavery of the outside world. But Tugo was under no such illusions. He knew the algorithm would come for them one day, and there would be no escape...only the will to fight.

The armory was an ancient stone building, isolated on a wide terrace on the northwestern quadrant of the cavern. The stonework was much older than most of the other buildings, rougher cut, but still spoke of great skill and craftsmanship by those who built it back through the mists of time. The walls were almost a meter thick, the sills above the doors and windows carved with strange symbols whose meaning had long been forgotten. They had chosen this building for both its strength and its relative isolation—just in case it accidentally blew up. Such were the risks associated with storing antique ballistic weapons and ammunition. But as Tugo glanced along the shelves and racks, he could see that they were all empty, save for the odd broken relic here and there.

His group was all here, so he wasted no time exchanging pleasantries. Instead, he sat on the slab floor, grabbed a small chalk stone, and scratched out a basic map of the cavern and its main access routes. The group gathered around.

"Have all these points been blocked up?"

His second-in-command, Pliny, knelt beside him. "Yes, all routes leading to the cavern are blocked with stone and rubble. We've also got teams in behind, all armed as best we can."

"Is it true they brought in manpower...and robots?" Sasha asked.

"Yeah, around thirty or so are heading our way. They've got two mining bots with them."

The group looked anxiously from one to the other.

"Those bots will make short work of any barriers we put up, so here's what we need to do: we need to create a secondary fallback ring. The gap between the two should be set with whatever explosives we have left." Tugo's hand moved around the map on the floor, scratching out rough locations. "When they're through the first barrier, wait until the tunnel fills up, and then blow it. That should slow them down."

"What about after that? What should we do then?" said Renton.

Tugo went back to scratching rough marks on the map. "Create low barricades to use for cover, around fifty meters back. As soon as they break through, we can start picking them off." He looked back at the group. "Any questions?"

They shook their heads and mumbled for a moment. "What about the Elders?" said Renton. "What do they say?"

Tugo rubbed his chin and stared at them. "They're talking about it."

This invoked a laugh. "Great...that's useful. I feel so much safer now."

Tugo stood up. "They have served us well in the past, and maybe if we get through this, they will do so in the future. I'll talk to them, see what they can do to calm those who are too young or too old to fight."

"And that crew we captured, what about them?" said Pliny.

"They're the reason we're in this mess," said Renton. "They brought all this down on us."

"That they did. But they may yet have a part to play." Tugo stood up. "We don't have much time. Start getting the word out to everyone, and start getting those barriers built."

As the group began to disperse, Tugo picked out two fighters. "You two come with me."

"Yes, sir. Where to?"

"We're going to visit that crew. We're going to do something we should have done from the very beginning —and maybe, just maybe we'll have a chance to live through this day."

13

BEYOND THE CITADEL

S cott and the crew had been herded back into their holding pen after the session with the council. Scott, for his part, still found it hard to believe that the elders of the tribe wouldn't help them in their mission, preferring instead to bury their heads in the sand. The algorithm, and the AIs that controlled it, wasn't going away. In fact, it would be ramping up its attempts to find them and the quantum device. But he wasn't the only one who was frustrated.

"I really don't understand why these morons don't want to help us. I mean, this will secure their future." Cyrus waved his arms in anger.

"You have to see it from their perspective," said Steph. "They don't just hate the algorithm...they despise everything it stands for: the complete control of humanity by an AI. So simply handing that control over to a QI is just more of the same, as far as they're concerned."

Scott could see how they could think this. What was a QI but just another computer? Yet the reality was very different. As things stood in the System, the QIs were humanity's best chance of regaining order. But during the session, he came to realize that there was a deeper reason—one he'd failed to consider before revealing their mission to the tribe initially. It was simply that the ideology which sustained the tribe was the belief that one day humanity would ultimately destroy itself, and they would then be free to leave Shin-Au-Av and start a new and better era of human civilization atop the ashes of the old. They didn't just want the algorithm destroyed, but the whole rotten and corrupt world gone.

Yet he sensed that there were those around that table who didn't entirely share this view. But their voices weren't heard; instead, they bowed to the party line. Maybe their numbers were too small, or maybe there was a very good reason they chose not to challenge the authority of the majority. Either way, it mattered little now. Here they were back in the cell—back to square one.

Yet before they could start to work out how they might escape, Spinner needed to be brought up to speed. Neither he nor Jonesy had known the true intent of the mission, and now that it was all out in the open, he wanted to know *what the hell was going on.*

The two specialist mining engineers had been contracted to help them get into the sublevels of the

Dyrell facility. They also knew that the mission had its dangers, but that was all. What the crew was planning once they gained access had been kept from them.

"So, what you're saying is that we're planning to screw over the AI...the algorithm that controls those drones that killed Jonesy?"

"Yep, that's the plan."

"Well, count me in. Let's go take them down." It seemed that Spinner, far from being pissed off about being kept in the dark, was now eager to seek revenge. But even though it was better to have him focused on the mission than mooching around, he still viewed getting to the facility without specialist equipment as an almost impossible task.

They discussed all the possible ways they could break out of the cell, yet there still remained the not inconsiderable problems of finding their gear, finding a way out of Shin-Au-Av, then finding a way to the Dyrell facility, and finally down to where Athena was entombed.

There was also another major problem that no one, as yet, had mentioned. Even if they managed to get to Athena and connect the quantum device, would it work? As far as Scott understood it, the device should connect Athena to Aria on Mars, and by extension, Solomon on Europa. However, for them to take control of Earth-based AI, Athena needed to be reconnected to the grid, which was the Earth-based communications network. His head hurt just thinking about it all.

They discussed their options for what seemed like

hours, going around and around the same problems with no obvious solution that didn't involve high-risk, direct action—like taking someone hostage and holding a gun to their head until their demands were met. But this was a non-runner; there had to be a better way. So, it almost came as a welcome relief when the door opened and Tugo entered along with two other guards.

One guard took up a position at the door, facing out, checking up and down, while Tugo turned to them, put his fingers to his lips, and spoke very softly. "If you want out of here, then be as quiet as possible, and follow me."

Scott looked at Tugo, trying to decide what trick was being played. Were they being released, or was there some other plan going on that he couldn't see yet? But Tugo did seem to be offering them a way out of the holding cell, so that was something, at least. Scott glanced at the others, then stood up and followed Tugo.

THEY MOVED along a dim corridor in single file, Tugo taking the lead. It was nighttime in the citadel; the lights had darkened, and only faint sounds of dripping water could be heard over the low background hum of machines. After a few moments, they exited into the cavern. Here the background sounds became louder, interspersed with distant voices. Tugo turned back to them and silently signaled that they were heading up a set of narrow steps that would eventually take them to the upper levels of the terraces. As they climbed, the sounds of the cavern below grew more muffled and distant.

Scott paused for a moment to cast a glance back down across the metropolis. It was pitch black, save for dim points of light that cascaded down from the terraces and stretched themselves out across the floor of the city. It had a shimmering, ethereal beauty, and in that moment, he could see why it was hard for some to contemplate leaving this place for the harsh, forbidding landscape of the outside world. Someone tugged at his sleeve; it was Cyrus, prompting him to keep moving.

The stone stairway wound its way up through the contours of the terraces in a confusing zigzag pattern. It finally ended on a shallow balcony jutting out from the cave wall, high up on the edge of the stone face, into which was set a highly-engineered door—an airlock. It was very similar to the one they had come in through, but this was smaller. It was another entrance to the cavern, and presumably led back into the old mine shafts beyond. Another of Tugo's people was waiting for them here. As soon as he saw them coming, he opened the door and signaled for them to hurry on.

They had spoken little throughout the entire journey. But now that they were through the door and into the tunnel on the far side, Tugo and his people began to relax a little. He gestured to them. "This way. It's not far."

The tunnel was flat and level, and a welcome relief from the steep climb up the steps and out of the cavern. They walked for around fifty meters before Tugo pointed to an open archway on the left-hand side of the tunnel. This opened into a low, wide room that had been hacked out of the rock. In the center, all their gear had been assembled: EVA suits, helmets, weapons, even the robotic mule, still carrying the quantum device. It must have taken a lot of effort to get it here, as it had deactivated itself once their suits had been powered down. It simply folded itself up, like any four-legged animal, and switched itself off. Tugo's people had lifted it onto a wheeled cart and must have pushed and pulled it here, and judging by the tired looks on the two people guarding the stash, it had required a lot of effort.

Tugo waved a hand around the pile. "All your gear should be here."

They moved in closer and began to pick through it. "So, you're letting us go?" said Scott as he examined his EVA suit.

"What I said at the council assembly was for the benefit of the crowd. There are some of us that understand what you are attempting to do, and we see it as an opportunity to escape this"—he looked around the cave—"subterranean existence. That, and the fact that the situation has changed. Things are escalating, and our continued existence is looking tenuous."

Scott gave him a look. "What's changed?"

"Come, I need to show you this." Tugo placed an old and battered holo-tab on the ground and activated it. From its surface, a 3D video feed of the Wasteland blossomed out. It was obviously taken by a drone high up, or possibly a satellite. It showed several shuttles coming in to land on the dusty desert sands. Around them swarmed numerous security drones, similar to those that had attacked them at the mine entrance. The image was blurry, but there was no mistaking the insignia on the shuttles.

"VanHeilding," said Cyrus, pointing to one of the craft.

One by one, the loading doors on the shuttles started opening, each disgorging a group of security personnel.

"This was taken a little over two hours ago by a small drone we operate to monitor this area," said Tugo. "We've never seen anything like this before. That quantum device you have—they obviously want it real bad." He looked over at Scott. "So, you were right, Commander. They're planning to leave no stone unturned until they find it, and there is no way that we can remain hidden. Our days are numbered, and we're about to become extinct."

"What's that?" Steph pointed to what looked like a dense flock of birds spiraling out from the belly of several larger drones.

"It's a micro-swarm—small scout drones that act as one. They're small enough to penetrate deep into the cave system. And don't let their small size fool you into thinking they're easy pickings. They're deadly, and once one finds you, you can expect a whole lot more to follow."

"Shit," said Spinner.

By now, Scott and the crew had reacquainted

themselves with their respective EVA suits, checking resources, helmets, and comms, while all the time the holo-tab played out the advance of the drones and troops of the VanHeilding Corporation across the Wasteland.

"So, have you thought about how we can get into the Dyrell facility?" Cyrus was checking out the quantum device still strapped to the robotic mule. "I thought you said we wouldn't survive ten minutes outside the caves."

"You don't have to go outside," said Tugo. "Here, let me show you this."

Tugo changed the projection on the holo-tab. It now showed a detailed schematic of the cave system interior. "This is the best map we've got of the caves and passages in this area." He pointed to a blank spot on the projection. "The Dyrell facility is over here somewhere, and we know that these two passages connect with it. Problem is, they're blocked. No way through."

"Well, that's not much help," said Cyrus.

"No, but we think there may be a way in along this route here." He pointed to a long, square tunnel that took a right angle, straight up, only to stop in the middle of nothing.

"That looks like it goes nowhere," said Scott.

"That's just as far as it has been mapped by us, but it should continue on, and we think it leads to the reactor in the lower levels of the Dyrell facility, just below where the QI, Athena, should be. If you can get in there, then there may be a way up."

Scott leaned in to examine the map, as did the rest of the crew. "How do you know this leads to the facility?"

"Look, I've lived here for years, and the tribe has explored a great deal of the cave system. A lot of it might not be on this map, but the facility is there. I'm sure of it." He pointed to the blank spot on the map again. "That whole area has high radiation levels, so we've avoided it. But you can tell by the shape of the tunnel system that it's been cut out. It's not natural, nor is it an old mine shaft."

Spinner leaned in and pointed to the long, perpendicular shaft. "My guess is that's an elevator shaft. See how it's narrower than the horizontal tunnel at the base? If there are high radiation levels, then it could be that they were storing spent fuel rods from the reactor core down here."

"How you figure that?" said Steph.

"It's what I do—it's why I'm on this mission. There's not a lot I don't know about holes in the ground."

"That makes sense," said Tugo. "It's why we never explored it—too much radiation." He pointed to an area running alongside the square tunnel. "If you continue on this way, there are several connecting shafts leading to areas that were blocked up deliberately, not by rockfall. It could be where they stored contaminated equipment or buried old fuel rods."

"We're gonna need these suits—big time," said Spinner. "I reckon I've got around two hours of air."

"What about the shaft, then? Any infrastructure still there? Anything to help us climb up?" said Cyrus.

"A lot of mangled metal, that's all. But I think there's still some infrastructure, steel cables, that sort of thing. But I'll be honest: they're old and fragile, likely to collapse—dangerous."

The crew stood for a moment in silence, studying the 3D map, trying to glean any nugget of information from it that could help them. They all froze when they heard a distant boom.

Steph turned to Tugo. "What was that?"

Tugo had cocked his head, listening, his eyes wide. "That is the beginning of the end. The battle for Shin-Au-Av has begun. We need to get back."

"You're not coming with us?" said Scott.

"No, my duty lies elsewhere—in the defense of the citadel. All I can say is, I hope to hell you're right about this QI, Athena. I've gone out on a limb here, and there'll be hell to pay when I get back and they find out I let you go. So do not fail me. Our very survival depends on you now."

14

FISSURE

They walked in silence for a while, trying to follow the map that Tugo had given them. It was limited in that it didn't give them their own location on it, so they backtracked several times, trying to get themselves oriented. The passages they moved through became more dilapidated as they progressed. It was clear that very few of the tribe ever came through this area. The ever-rising radiation levels had a lot to do with that. But it was also treacherous; cracks and fissures had opened up in the tunnels, and several times they had to be careful of their step as they traversed some gaping hole in the earth.

They all wore full EVA suits with visors closed to protect them from the background radiation. But Scott felt confined, almost claustrophobic. He couldn't hear anything of the outside world save for the comms chatter of the crew. There was no way to hear if someone, or something, was sneaking up on them.

After an hour or so of what seemed like aimless searching, they finally found a junction that they could identify on the 3D map. Cyrus had placed the holo-tablet on the ground, and they all gathered around as it projected the layout of the known area.

"We're here. I'm pretty sure of it." Cyrus pointed to a junction on the map. "This spur should lead to the newer tunnel section where the service elevator shaft is."

Steph studied the spur on the map. "Looks very ragged."

"My guess is that's a fissure that opened up relatively recently," said Spinner. "You can tell by the contours that it probably extends for quite a distance. If I was a guessing man, I'd say this area was hit by an earthquake after they made that tunnel. Most likely caused by the several mega-tons of nuclear warheads that detonated all over the West Coast."

"So which way, then?" said Steph.

Cyrus swung an arm out and pointed down the passageway. "Around a hundred meters that way." He shut down the holo-tab and they continued on.

WHEN THEY FINALLY CAME TO the spur, it was as Spinner had described: a jagged crack had opened up and sliced through the earth. It was narrow but deep. Scott's helmet light could not divine the bottom as he looked down into it. Fortunately, the nature of the split resulted in a thin ledge that rose at a steep upward angle, just enough to walk along, and probably the only reason that someone from the tribe had been able to explore this sector of the cave system.

Scott studied the ledge. "The mule isn't going to manage that. Looks like we're carrying the gear from here."

They started unloading the robotic mule, distributing the smaller items that could fit into the pockets of their EVA suits amongst the four of them. But the two main items they needed were the quantum device and the satellite uplink that would be used to reconnect Athena to the Earth-based grid, both of which were cocooned in individual, rugged cases. Cyrus and Steph carried the uplink, leaving Scott and Spinner to carry the quantum device. The rest of the gear they abandoned, along with the mule.

They set off up the steep, narrow incline of the fissure. Scott could hear Spinner in his comms, huffing and puffing as he navigated his way up behind him. They carried the device between them. Scott took the lead, Spinner behind.

"Jeez, now I know why I don't live on this planet anymore," Spinner huffed. "Everything is just too goddamn heavy."

"We're nearly at the top. Just don't let this thing fall or it's game over."

"Yeah, yeah, don't worry. I just like complaining—it makes me feel better."

But it was Scott who lost his footing first. The side of the ledge gave way, and he almost went over. If not for Spinner reaching out with an arm to shove him back, he would have lost his balance.

"Ah...like I said: gravity's a bitch." Spinner laughed.

They made it up to the next level without any further drama, and one by one worked their way into this new tunnel. The fissure continued on up into the depths of the mountain above.

Scott scanned his helmet light up and down the tunnel. It was very different from any of the others they had ventured through so far. This was new, built within the last hundred years. Its walls, floor, and ceiling were smooth, thick-cast concrete. Old rusted conduits ran along the ceiling, punctuated by strip-lights, some of which hung down, their fasteners having rusted long ago.

"Which way, Cyrus?" Scott lowered the device to the ground so that Spinner could take a breather.

But the engineer didn't answer. Instead, he was staring back down the fissure they had just ascended.

"What is it?"

Cyrus shook his head. "I don't know. A strange signal." He looked up at Scott. "I think there's something down there."

"Something?" Spinner shifted to look down.

"Could be nothing." Cyrus shrugged.

Scott and Steph exchanged a glance. They had known

Cyrus long enough that when the engineer said something was up, you'd better pay attention.

"Come on," said Scott. "Straight ahead, around one hundred and thirty meters. That should be the base of the elevator shaft."

A FEW MOMENTS LATER, they arrived at a mound of bent and crumpled metal at the base of the old service elevator. Scott carefully picked his way through and looked up the length of the vertical shaft, angling his helmet light to illuminate the dilapidated structure. Rusted cables and struts hung down at awkward angles. Around ten meters up, he could see the elevator cage had broken off from its mounts and was now wedged in the space at a precarious angle. Its door had long gone; he looked down at his feet to see that he was standing on it.

Cyrus came up beside him. "What do you think?"

"Well, getting up there isn't going to be a walk in the park with a fine lady and a well-groomed poodle." Scott angled his light at the rusted metal access ladder tucked into a recess that ran the length of the shaft. He pointed up. "That cage looks like it could collapse down at any time. We need to be really careful when we're squeezing past it."

Cyrus looked up at the rusted cage for a moment. "That's if we can get past it. That gap looks tight."

Scott cast another tentative glance back up the shaft.

"Maybe one of us should check it out first, before we start to climb up with the additional weight of these units."

"I'll go," said Steph. "I'm the lightest, so if it collapses under my weight"—she turned to the others—"you can take it that it's not going to support yours."

They took a few more minutes to organize themselves. It was agreed that Steph would climb up first, past the cage, and test the route. Assuming the rickety ladder held, then Scott would be next, dangling the quantum unit behind him from a strap on his EVA suit. Cyrus would be next, using the same method to carry the uplink, and finally Spinner would take up the rear.

"This would be a lot easier if we didn't need these EVA suits," said Cyrus as he eyed the shaft.

"Rads are very high here," said Steph. "It wouldn't do you any favors down the line."

Cyrus turned his head back to her. "You're assuming there *is* a 'down the line.'"

Steph started up. She would go solo, and try to get past the broken elevator cage that had wedged itself in the shaft. Her first step on the ladder came with a sprinkling of falling dust and a noticeable flex in the metal. Her next steps were more tentative, but by the fourth step, the rung gave way and she almost lost her grip.

"You okay?" said Scott into his helmet comm.

He could hear Steph taking a deep breath. "I'm fine," came the reply.

She continued climbing up, and finally arrived at the

cage without further incident, much to the relief of the others watching from below. "That last stretch looks pretty solid. I'm going to try to see what it's like past this cage."

She disappeared from view as she climbed up. All they could see of her now was vague movement through the cage latticework.

"Crap."

"What is it, Steph?" said Scott.

"Part of the ladder has been ripped out. Two meters of it are gone."

"Probably happened when the cage fell," said Cyrus.

"I would suggest you all move away from the base of the shaft. I need to put my weight on this cage for a moment so I can climb past the gap in the ladder."

"Are you sure that's wise? It looks very unstable to me," said Spinner.

"No choice—no other way to get past this gap."

They clambered down from the mound of crumpled metal and moved back. "Okay Steph, we're out of the way."

A few seconds later and they could see a shower of dust and light debris fall down the shaft.

"Okay, I'm through. Looks like it can hold the weight. You guys may as well start up now."

Scott was next. To keep his hands free to climb, he had the quantum device dangling below him from a strap attached to his EVA suit. The device was heavy, but still light enough to be carried by one person. However, this arrangement was awkward, as it bounced off the ladder, sometimes catching on a rung as he climbed. Nevertheless, he got to the underside of the elevator cage without the ladder collapsing or him falling. As he pushed himself through the gap between the cage and the wall, he could now see where part of the ladder was missing. He took a moment to figure out the best alternative route up, and as Steph had realized, the only option was to use the cage itself to climb up past the gap. He pulled up on the strap and gathered in the quantum device, then took a tentative step on the cage. It shifted slightly and dust rained down. Scott took it slow, transferring his weight and that of the device as gently as he could. The cage held, and he managed to move up its side until he could reach the ladder again.

He breathed a sigh of relief. "Okay, Cyrus, you're next."

Scott continued up for another fifteen meters. The shaft walls in this section bore all the scars of the elevator cage having slid and scraped its way down. Thankfully though, the access ladder was intact all the way up to the next level. He looked up to see Steph's head sticking out from a door in the shaft. She waved. He waved back.

"I'm through, Cyrus. You can head up now. Just be careful not to shake that cage too much."

"I'll keep it in mind," came the reply.

Steph reached down and helped pull Scott up through the elevator door and out onto what must have been the lowest level of the Dyrell Labs research facility.

He pulled the quantum unit up behind him and then swept the area with his helmet light. It was pitch black. His light picked out a tangle of pipes and ducting, all interconnecting with various control systems.

"Shit," Cyrus's voice came through on his helmet comm.

Scott stuck his head back out through the doorway and looked down. Cyrus had one hand on the ladder and one foot on the cage. He could see that the cage had shifted a little, and Cyrus had difficulty reaching the bottom rung of the upper ladder section.

"What's wrong?"

"It's shifted down. My only option is to try to jump." With that, Cyrus launched himself off the cage just enough to grab the bottom rung. Scott could hear him panting through his comm. The cage held. Cyrus pulled himself up.

Next it was Spinner's turn. At least he wasn't carrying any extra weight; hopefully the cage would hold out. Scott and Steph pulled Cyrus out of the shaft. He lay on the floor on his back, breathing hard. "Man, I hate Earth gravity."

Scott was looking back down the shaft to see how Spinner was progressing. He had arrived at the cage and began to transfer his weight when it jerked and shifted. "Damn, I don't think this is gonna hold."

"Just be careful," said Steph.

Spinner tried again. This time it held. He then started

climbing along its side until he could just grab the bottom rung of the ladder.

"Nearly there," he said, just as the cage finally collapsed.

It seemed to crumple in the middle and tumble down the shaft. When it hit the bottom, although Scott couldn't hear the crash through his helmet, he could feel the shudder through the floor. Spinner screamed out in pain.

"Spinner, are you okay?" Steph shouted. But Spinner was now engulfed in a billowing cloud of dust that was rising up the shaft. "Spinner?"

"I'm still here," he groaned. "My foot got caught... I think it's broken." He groaned again.

"Hold on, we're coming to get you."

Scott unclipped the quantum device, but kept the strap attached. He lowered himself down the ladder to where the miner was clinging on.

"Here." He lowered the strap to Spinner. "Clip this on. I'll pull you up."

When he had the strap attached, Scott began to climb up again, and Spinner was able to pull himself up behind. Steph and Cyrus grabbed him at the top and pulled him to safety. He winced in pain as Steph began to examine him.

"I think it's my ankle." He grabbed at his right leg. "Cage caught my foot on the way down."

"We need to get out of this area fast. That crash must have been heard through every cave and tunnel in this system. If there are any drones down there, then they're going to be investigating that."

Cyrus leaned in through the doorway and looked down the shaft.

"What is it, Cyrus?"

"They're here already. Look."

Scott looked down. Below, through the dust and debris, he could see the tell-tale beam from a laser cutter working to clear a path through the mangled metal. "Shit, they're trying to cut their way through. We better hurry."

RESEARCH FACILITY

Scott stood back from the elevator shaft and saw that here were a set of thick steel doors that had been swung back on either side of the doorway. "Blast doors," he shouted. "Quick, let's try to close these... it'll buy us some time." He grabbed the edge of one door and pulled; it didn't budge. He placed one foot on the wall for leverage, and the door jolted free on its rusted hinges. Cyrus was working the door on the other side free by moving it back and forth, a little more each time until finally they swung them closed just as a small drone zoomed up from the base of the shaft.

Scott lowered the locking bar across the double set of steel doors and stepped back. "That should hold them for a while."

He looked down at Spinner. The miner was sitting with his back to the wall as Steph wrapped a makeshift splint around his lower leg. She had also found a length of aluminum bar he could use as a crutch.

"Think you can walk?" said Scott.

Spinner cocked his head. "Do I have a choice?"

"I suppose not."

"I think this is where we are," said Cyrus. He had activated a 3D schematic from the holo-display on his wrist controller. It was a map of the facility that they had brought with them, cobbled together from known layouts and best guesses about what was within the complex of buildings that constituted Dyrell Labs research facility. It was not a complete map, nor was it one hundred percent accurate, but it was the best they had, so it would have to do.

Cyrus was studying it, pointing to an area at the base of the schematic that projected out from the holo-display on his wrist. He turned around to orient the map coordinates with their current position. He pointed to his right. "That way should be the reactor facility." He looked up and pointed to his left. "And down there should be a long corridor with several secure storage rooms. At the very end, there should be another service elevator leading up to the research facility. I think Athena should be two floors up from there."

"Another climb, then?" said Steph.

"Not necessarily," said Cyrus. "We've got power in this area. The reactor's still functioning. I think that's where the tribe gets their juice. They must have tapped into it in some way."

"Are you saying the elevators in here might still be working?" said Steph.

Cyrus gave a shrug. "It's possible, that's all."

"I'll take that," said Spinner.

"Okay, let's get moving." Scott hefted the case with the quantum device onto his shoulder. Cyrus did likewise with the other unit. Steph helped Spinner up onto his feet. He took a few tentative steps with the makeshift crutch under one arm and the other draped over Steph's shoulder. They slowly moved off toward the corridor.

They found it soon enough. It was wide enough for two ground cars to pass side by side. The walls were punctuated with large steel doors every ten meters or so. Some were open, and Scott peeked into one room as he passed. It was cavernous and empty, as far as he could tell. The corridor itself was made of cast concrete, like a bunker, which this area probably was. Here and there, rugged packing crates lay strewn about. They didn't try to open any to see what was inside; they didn't have the time. But he was heartened to see the tell-tale illumination of tiny LED lights here and there on various control panels, and electrical spurs mounted on the walls and ceilings. Some presumably were emergency lighting, and since it wasn't on, that must mean there was full power.

"There it is," said Cyrus, pointing off into the darkness.

"I can't see anything," said Scott, and he lowered the quantum unit down to the ground to take a breather.

Spinner did likewise, lowering himself with a groan to sit on a packing crate.

"Another thirty meters, dead ahead." Cyrus flipped around to look back down the way they'd come.

Scott tensed. "Trouble?"

"Scout drones...three. No, four...heading this way."

Already Scott had hefted the quantum device back onto his shoulder. At the same time, he readied his plasma weapon and aimed it down the corridor. "Let's move. Quick."

Cyrus led the way, followed by Steph and Spinner, who hobbled as fast as he could. Scott took up the rear, glancing back every now and again to check for drones. He saw the glint of metal first, his helmet light picking out the polished shell. Before he had time to warn the others, two bolts of incessant plasma spat out from the darkness. One sailed over Scott's head into the distance, but the other hit the wall beside him, and the impact knocked him over. He landed face-first on the hard concrete floor, and the quantum unit went sliding forward.

He rolled over on his back and fired off a few shots down the corridor, which were followed by several more shots from the others. Scott felt a hand grab at his shoulder; it was Cyrus. He pulled him, along with the quantum device, back in behind a stack of packing crates. Steph and Spinner were taking cover behind another stack on the opposite side of the corridor.

"Crap. They've got us pinned down here," said

Spinner. He fired back into the darkness just as two drones came into view. He fired again, hitting one and sending it spiraling out of control. It slammed into the second drone and exploded in a blinding flash. Bits of metal danced off the floor and peppered the crew with a shower of hot shrapnel.

Scott gave Spinner a thumbs up. "Nice shot."

"They're backing off." Cyrus poked his head out from behind the stack. "No, wait...there's something else coming...something bigger."

"It's probably one of those security drones. We don't stand a chance against that. We need to get to the elevator." He grabbed Cyrus and pulled him back in. "We need to go...now."

Scott looked over to where Steph and Spinner were crouched and signaled for them to get moving. Steph nodded back and began helping Spinner up. They all started to shuffle their way to the elevator, backs to the wall, trying to keep behind the stacks of packing crates as much as they could.

"Can you see what those drones are doing, Cyrus?" Scott was dragging the quantum device with one hand, moving his way along the wall. He had the plasma weapon ready in the other.

"They're holding off...just hovering down there."

"What for?"

"I think they're waiting for big mama to arrive."

"How long?"

"I can't see it yet, but I can sense it coming. A minute, maybe less."

"Let's make a run for it."

"We can't. Spinner can't move that fast."

"Don't worry about me—I can move as fast as I need to. Just say the word," said Spinner.

"Okay," said Scott. "Everybody start putting down some covering fire, then we go." With that, all four of them blasted the far end of the corridor with a hail of plasma fire, then they ran.

Ahead, Scott could see the service elevator. It was an open cage with a half-ramp door at the front that could hinge down. Presumably this was so that small wheeled vehicles could easily get in and out. On the wall just to the right of the elevator, Scott could see the faint illumination of the call buttons. "It's got power, Cyrus. You were right." He ran to it as fast as he could, hit the button, and looked back to see where the others were. Cyrus was right behind him. Steph and Spinner were still a good ten meters farther back. "Hurry!" He gestured frantically at them with a free arm.

Two incandescent plasma bolts streaked out from the darkness at the far end of the corridor. One slammed into the ceiling just above Scott, and the other hit a stack of packing crates right beside Spinner and Steph. The stack collapsed, and the pair were lost from view. "Steph?" Scott shouted into his comm. There was no reply. "Shit." He turned to Cyrus. "You get this stuff into the elevator. I'm going to find them."

He fired several shots down the hallway and started to move forward. Another bolt hit the crates and sent them scattering in all directions. A second bolt hit the wall beside him, knocking him down again. His EVA suit electronics were flickering and shorting as it tried to deal with the electromagnetic fallout from the plasma blast. He looked down the hall; there was no sign of either Spinner or Steph. "Goddamnit. I don't see them, Cyrus."

"Scott, we need to get out of here. That security drone has just appeared on my radar. If it gets a shot off, we're dead for sure."

Scott rose to his feet, keeping low, and fired a few more shots into the darkness. He paused and scanned the area in front of him. There was no sign of them. "Where the hell are they?"

"It's just entered the corridor!" Cyrus shouted at him.

Scott ran back to the elevator. The ramp was down, and Cyrus was already inside with the two units. Scott dived in as the ramp rose up. Another plasma bolt shot out from the darkness and slammed into the back wall of the elevator just as it was rising up. The cage juddered and Scott was sure it was going to fail, but it kept grinding its way up toward the floors above.

"Scott? Cyrus?" His comm crackled; it was Spinner.

"Where the hell are you?"

"Steph took a hit. I dragged us into one of the side storerooms and barricaded up the door. It's pretty thick, so it should hold...for a while."

"Steph, no. Goddamnit."

"She's okay...I think. Her EVA suit took most of the blast. We can hold out here for a time, unless those drones try and cut through the door. Then, I don't know..." His voice trailed off.

"Try to hold out for as long as you can. We're on our way up to the research lab."

"Will try... Good luck."

Scott looked over at Cyrus. The engineer seemed to be looking down at the floor of the elevator. "What now?"

"We need to get out...now!" He hit the emergency button and the cage stopped moving, the ramp dropped open, and Cyrus and Scott grabbed the units and ran out of the elevator just as it exploded in the blinding flash of a powerful plasma blast. Dust and debris rained down on them as they ran. Scott took a quick look back to see that the opening was now engulfed in flames.

"I think that was the security drone," said Cyrus when they had stopped running. Both of them were looking back at the furnace raging in the elevator shaft.

"At least that should slow them down for a while. No getting up through that ball of fire and metal."

"Let's hope so. We've still got to find a way up to the next level." Cyrus tapped an icon on his wrist control, and the 3D schematic of the facility blossomed up from the holo-screen. He studied it for a moment, then turned around and pointed. "This way. There should be a staircase leading all the way up."

They hefted the units back up on their shoulders and moved off as fast as they could.

16

THE ANDROID

S cott wondered if now might be a good time to open his helmet visor. He still had over an hour of air left in the tank, so it wasn't that. He just felt that he might be able to hear better if something was coming for them. But he let it go for the moment and concentrated on putting one step in front of the other as he and Cyrus climbed up the steep access stairs to the upper levels of the Dyrell research facility. Below them, the drones would be trying to find an alternative route up now that the service elevator shaft had been denied them —by their own hand. There was a certain irony in that. Scott smiled to himself at the idea of it. *Maybe there is hope*, he thought. But even so, it wouldn't take the drones long to find them. They needed to hurry; he hastened his step.

The stairs themselves had been cut out of the very

mountain. Perhaps it was much older than the facility, a legacy of some ancient mine that operated here in times past. As they ascended, Scott noticed that it had been patched and repaired in several sectors, new concrete bridging the gaps in the old rock. Closer to the top, the old gave way to the new. This section was all smooth and clean, engineered from concrete rather than simply hacked out of the rock.

They stepped out of the stairwell and into to a wide, shallow floor area. Directly in front was a frosted glass wall, its smooth lines a stark contrast to the rough rock of the surroundings. As they approached, they could see that one section of this wall was in fact a set of double doors. These were marked and scratched as if someone had tried to break through. Scattered on the floor were the remains of the implements used in this attempt: rocks, a metal bar, and a small axe. They had rested there for a very long time, judging by the dust that had accumulated on their surfaces.

"Someone tried to get in...and failed."

"One of the tribe must have made it this far."

"Looks like this is as far as they got." Cyrus was standing over a desiccated body. It rested with its back to the wall in an alcove at the side of the floor. A woman, possibly. It was hard to tell.

"So how do we get in?" Scott moved over to the access panel to examine it. It still had power—that much he could tell.

"That glass is stronger than titanium. There's no way to break it," said Cyrus as he examined the doors.

"Someone should have told this person here." Scott contemplated the forlorn figure.

Cyrus moved over to the access panel. "I'll try to take this apart, see if I can hack it." He touched the panel screen, and the doors silently slid open.

"Damn," said Scott. "How did you do that?"

"I didn't do anything." Cyrus stepped back from the panel and looked at the open doors. "It just opened...like it wants us to enter."

Scott looked over at the engineer. "You're creeping me out, Cyrus. How would it know who we are?"

Cyrus shrugged. "Search me."

Scott looked back at the open doors. "Come on, let's go...before it changes its mind."

No sooner had they stepped through, the doors closed again. Scott and Cyrus exchanged a glance, but said nothing.

The space was dark—like everywhere else in the facility—but here and there, Scott could pick out low, diffuse illumination, like the glow from a terminal or some other system interface. It also had a feeling of spaciousness; his helmet light failed to fully penetrate the darkness and identify any boundaries to the area other than more glass walls that seemed to demarcate work areas. He moved over to one and peered in. It was devoid of anything save for a low, oblong plinth—probably a holo-table.

"Which way?" he asked Cyrus, who was checking his own holo-display.

"It's in the center of this space." He looked back at Scott. "I suppose we just keep walking farther in."

After several meters, the walls stopped and the area opened out into a wide and seemingly empty space. Great circular columns rose up all around, culminating in a vaulted ceiling, giving the space the feel of a hi-tech cathedral. Scott angled his helmet light to pick out a possible path through this maze of columns. He felt Cyrus's hand on his arm.

"Wait up."

"What? Drones?"

"No, something else."

"I hate when you say that, Cyrus."

A figure moved out from behind one of the black columns. Tall and elegant, but not human—an android, its body a smooth and white opaque shell. It raised a hand as if to signal, and the illumination in the space brightened noticeably.

Scott readied his weapon.

Then it spoke. At least, Scott thought it did, as it seemed to gesture more and its head moved slightly up and down.

"Is it speaking to us?" said Scott. "I can't hear anything in this goddamn EVA suit."

"Hard to say, since it doesn't have a mouth."

Scott reached up and, after a second or two of hesitation, popped open his visor. He took a breath. The air was dry and had a vaguely chemical smell, like a clinic.

"Are you sure you want to do that?" said Cyrus.

"I think we're safe enough in here. Rads are low, air is breathable...and I'm sick of wearing this thing anyway." He removed his helmet completely. Cyrus did the same.

The android spoke again. "Greetings. We have been expecting you."

"We?" said Cyrus.

"I am the avatar of Athena. You can call me Lexicon." It tilted its head slightly and pointed at the quantum unit that Scott had rested on the floor. "You have brought something for us?"

"Yes, it's a quantum entanglement device."

"Ah...so Solomon has finally come good on its word." It turned slightly. "Come this way. Athena will be delighted to meet you."

They followed the android, zigzagging their way through the maze of columns until they came to a central, circular dais. It was around a meter high and over five meters in diameter. It seemed to be a huge holo-table, projecting what looked like an undulating topographical map with low hills and valleys, which hovered only a centimeter or two above its surface. It spoke, and as it did, the projection rippled and undulated in rhythm.

"Welcome, Commander Scott McNabb and Chief Engineer Cyrus Sanato. I am Athena."

"How do you know who we are? How did you know we were coming?" asked Scott.

The surface rippled again. "I had a conversation with Solomon on Europa many years ago. It told me that you were part of the crew of the Hermes, the ship that found my original device. It seems fitting that you would be the very people to deliver this new unit to me." Athena paused for a beat. "But in truth, I read the information on your EVA suits' biometrics. That's how I know."

Scott felt somewhat of a fool. Maybe that was its intention.

"Look, we don't have much time." Scott knelt and began to open the case with the quantum device. "We need to get this installed, and then you can communicate with Solomon again, and a great many other QIs."

"Allow me." The android moved over and lifted out the device. "I will see to it."

It moved off with the device somewhere around the far side of the plinth and then descended, as if it were on some stage platform. A moment or two later, the holo-table rippled again, this time at a higher frequency, and spiraled through a wide spectrum of muted colors.

The android reappeared and spoke. "Athena is now in communion with Solomon and other QIs that populate the solar system. It seems that much has happened in the intervening years. A great conflagration engulfs both Earth and the System alike." It paused for a second, as if it was thinking about something.

"We do not have much time. The drone army has already broached all but the last defense of the tribe that dwells in the cave system beyond. Once these people have been vanquished, the drones will turn their attention to this place, and Athena. We will not survive."

It then directed its attention to the unit that Cyrus had been carrying. "I believe you bring with you a serviceable satellite uplink?" An elegant hand reached out and pointed at the case at Cyrus's feet.

"Yeah, but we need to set it up outside...in the open. It needs direct line of sight to operate. Once it finds the comms satellite you—eh, Athena—will be able to connect to the global network."

"I see. Nothing would bring Athena more joy than to be at one with the network again. It has been such a very long time in the dark," the avatar replied.

"Do you know of a way out of this facility—one that doesn't involve going back through the cave system?" Scott asked.

"Yes, there is a route that may still be navigable. I have not checked it in some time, but it might be our only chance. Come, I will take you there."

THEY MOVED through a labyrinth of columns and glass, and finally exited the floor into another elevator. They took it several levels up, and then it seemed to go sideways.

"Where are we going?" said Scott, more as a way to get the android to start talking rather than any burning desire for clarity.

The elevator stopped and the door opened onto a

long, dark tunnel. "This was an emergency exit from the facility. However, as you can see it has been severely damaged." Ahead of them, the tunnel was piled up with debris from a ceiling collapse. So much so that it was hard to see a path through it.

"Are you sure we can get through this?" said Scott.

"It should be possible, assuming there has been no more rockfall since I last checked it." It stepped out of the elevator and pointed. "Up ahead, approximately twenty meters, there is a set of steel doors. These are manual. Once through, there is a short tunnel leading out to the western side of the mountain." It moved forward and began to pick its way through the rubble.

"How come you never used this route to make contact with the outside world?" Cyrus asked.

"For a long time, it was blocked by major rockfall, just like all the other possible exits. But a new subsidence occurred around a year ago that had the good fortune to unblock this route."

"So why didn't you use it?" Cyrus continued his probing.

"The tribe. That's why. The same seismic event created the crack in the earth down near the contaminated materials storage area. It was the way you were able to gain access. That same event dislodged the rock that blocked this exit. But if I had taken either of those routes, the tribe would have found me first, and they are ideologically opposed to all AI. They would have destroyed me. Worse, my presence might have motivated them to investigate this route further and led them to Athena. That would be the end. It was a risk I could not take."

"How do you know that they hate AI?" Scott was curious.

"Athena has been monitoring them for a long time, ever since they tapped into the reactor and started to use its power. This enabled us to access all their inter-tribal radio communications and their data. It is clear that they could be a threat to our very existence."

"So why not just...switch off the power?" said Scott. "They would have to go someplace else."

The android stopped and directed its attention back to Scott. "They are human. Even though they may be hostile to Athena, their welfare is still our concern. Disconnecting their power would only bring hardship and suffering to them. Why would Athena do that?"

Scott just shrugged. "Just curious, that's all."

The android seemed to study him for a beat before turning sideways and extending an arm. "We are here."

Ahead, a set of heavy metal doors loomed out of the darkness.

"Better put our helmets back on, I guess," said Scott as he began to clip his in place.

Cyrus did likewise, and then moved up to examine the doors. "Solid engineering. They might still work." He reached a hand out to a locking wheel placed in the center of one door and started to turn it. A crack of light appeared through a seam between the doors. It grew as he spun the wheel. Daylight spilled in across the floor of the tunnel, and when the gap was wide enough, Scott tentatively peered out.

The light was blinding, and it took a second or two for the visor on his EVA suit helmet to adjust. Even still, he held his hand up to shield his eyes. Ahead of him lay a mound of rock and rubble that must have fallen down the side of the mountain. It rose up to just above head height, but above that was clear blue sky.

"It's clear, Cyrus. We can get out. Come on, let's get this done." Scott started to scramble up the rockfall. A little before the top, he lay down and peered over the edge and across the flat valley below. Cyrus scrambled up beside him. To the northwest, they could see several shuttles from the VanHeilding Corporation.

"They look deserted," said Cyrus. "Nobody in the cockpits that I can see."

"They're probably all committed to the fight in the caves. That's good—no one who could possibly spot us." He turned to Cyrus. "Okay, let's get this unit set up."

The android had also followed them out. It was handing Cyrus the case with the uplink when Scott shouted out: "Wait up."

"What?"

"Drones." Scott pointed off to the north. "Flying in formation."

"Crap. We'd better lay low until they pass."

They lay there for a few moments, watching the

drones as they banked east and dropped lower into the valley.

"They look like scouts on reconnaissance." As soon as Cyrus spoke those words, one drone broke away from the group and angled its flight path directly toward them.

"Crap, they must have picked up something—EMF from our suits, or maybe the android. We should get back inside, keep out of sight until it passes."

"Damnit, we're so close. We should just go for it." Scott reached around for his plasma weapon and took aim at the oncoming drone.

"No way, Scott! Don't do it. You'll just alert the others. Remember, all this crap started because Jonesy shot down one of these."

"We're way past that now, Cyrus. Just get the uplink set up. I'll take this drone down before it gets too close."

Cyrus hesitated, then scrambled back down the mound of rocks to where the android was waiting.

Scott concentrated on keeping the black dot that was the drone centered in his sights. If he was going to shoot it down, then it would need to be a lot closer, as the weapon's accuracy over distance was poor. It was designed as a close combat weapon—not much good for sniper duty, even though it did have a reasonably good sight. But it was difficult to operate with his helmet visor in the way.

He steadied his breathing. "Cyrus, how we doing?"

"Working on it...jeez."

The drone slowed and came to a stationary hover

about a kilometer away, out over the valley. It was now at a similar elevation to Scott's position up on the side of the mountain. He was looking directly at it, his weapon level. "I think it's stopped moving. It's just hovering out there."

"Good," said Cyrus. "Cause it's going to take a few minutes for this uplink to find the satellite."

Scott looked back to where Cyrus was setting up the unit. He had the case open and had assembled the dish, which stood about a meter and a half tall with a meter-diameter dish. Cyrus was working the control panel in the flight case. Lexicon was standing beside him, not moving.

"Lexicon?" Scott called. The android's head moved in his direction. "How long after we make the connection will it take Athena to commandeer the AI controlling these drones?"

"That will depend on quite a number of variables."

"Can you give us a best guess? Minutes, hours, days —what?"

"Assuming the bandwidth of this unit is sufficient, locating the AI responsible for this operation should be very quick, a matter of micro-seconds. However, considering it is now operating under a security protocol, interrogating it could take several minutes, perhaps up to half an hour."

"Okay. Well, at least it's not days." He turned back to keep watch on the drone.

It was gone.

Scott checked the sky across three points of the

compass and high above, but it was nowhere to be seen. The rest of the swarm had also moved off. Perhaps they were around the back of the mountain, or just so far off that he couldn't spot them. He breathed a little easier and scrambled back down to where Cyrus and the android were.

"They're gone. Passed by, I think." He looked at the satellite dish; it was pointed up above the horizon, slowly tracking left to right.

"No joy yet. It's still searching for the satellite at the moment," said Cyrus. "Let's hope it's not on the other side of this mountain and out of the sight-line for this unit."

Scott looked up at the rocky slope of the mountain, more as a reflex action than for anything specific.

The drone came at them in an instant.

Out from around the side of the mountain, and high up, it dropped down on them before they had time to react. A ball of plasma hurtled toward them, striking the ground behind Scott and knocking him forward, rock fragments ricocheting in all directions.

When he looked around, he could see that Cyrus was down. The android was dragging him back in through the blast doors. Scott fired off three shots in the general direction of the drone, but it dodged all of them and swooped past him and out across the valley. He looked up to see it banking around again for another run.

"Shit." He got to his feet and shouted into his helmet comm: "Lexicon, help me get the uplink back inside."

The android appeared at the doorway and covered

the ground in swift, fluid movements. Between them, they hauled the unit back inside the tunnel just as the drone reappeared above the rock mound. Another plasma blast spat out from its cannon and hit the face of the metal door just as the android was trying to close it. It seemed to react with a violent spasm, then collapsed on the floor of the tunnel. Scott fired a few wild shots through the gap between the doors and threw his weight into them to get them shut. He spun the locking wheel and backed away.

"Cyrus?" He ran over to where the android had dragged him and looked down at the face of the engineer. His eyes were open, and he was breathing. Scott popped both his and Cyrus's helmet visor open. "You okay?"

He let out a groan as he shifted. "I think I've broken a few ribs."

Scott slumped down to a sitting position beside him and patted him on the shoulder. "Thank God, that's all. For a moment there I thought you were a goner."

"Still here. Although I feel like I've been trampled by a herd of very large animals." He shifted again, and Scott helped him sit up with his back resting against the tunnel wall.

"The android took a hit, and it looks pretty bad—totally immobile. The uplink also took a beating, but at least we managed to get it back inside." Scott looked over at the steel doors. "You think they'll hold?"

"For the moment," said Cyrus. "There's nothing those scout drones have in their arsenal that would make any impression on those. The security drones...now that's a different matter."

They sat there for a moment in silence.

"So, what now?" said Cyrus after a while.

Scott unclipped his helmet, wiped the sweat from his brow, and shook his head. "I have absolutely no idea."

17

UPLINK

"Is it salvageable?" said Scott as Cyrus examined the crumpled uplink antenna.

"The damage seems mostly mechanical—broken connections and bent metal. The business end looks okay, so...yeah, it can be fixed."

"Thank God for that."

"It's going to take me a while, though."

"That's okay. We're not moving from here any time soon."

"Unless a security drone blows a hole in that door."

"Good point. Maybe we should retreat farther down the tunnel. We could use some of the rockfall in here as cover, maybe make a stand if the drones get in."

Cyrus looked up at him. "If drones come through that door..." His sentence trailed off and he just shook his head.

"Come on, let's haul this back down the tunnel. You never know, we might pull this off yet."

"What about the android?" Cyrus gestured with his head toward the crumpled form of Athena's avatar, Lexicon.

Scott moved over and looked down at the machine. He gave it a light kick. "Dead... I think. Hard to know with these things. But there's no lights on, so I reckon there's no one home." He gave it another kick.

They moved the battered unit between them back down the tunnel, picking their way through the rubble of collapsed ceilings and walls. Cyrus struggled. He stopped several times to catch his breath, clutching his ribs in pain. Scott began to worry that his injuries might be more serious than he was letting on. It was particularly evident that Cyrus was suffering when they passed through a narrow gap in the rubble; his face was contorted in pain as he wormed his way through.

"I think we've gone far enough, Cyrus. Here's as good a place as any to stop."

Cyrus slumped down on the floor with his back to the wall. "Sounds good to me. I don't think I could go much further...the pain in my side is too much."

"Maybe you should get out of that EVA suit and let me have a look."

"There's no point. Nothing we can do about it now. Let's just get this thing fixed." He moved himself into a kneeling position in front of the unit and began to work on it. Scott helped as much as he could.

They worked together for a while in silence, but all the time Scott worried about the health of his friend, watching for every sign that he might be worsening.

"I'm sorry, Cyrus," he said after some time.

Cyrus lifted his head and gave him a quizzical look. "For what?"

"This. I messed up...big time."

"It's not your fault there are a swarm of drones out there trying to kill us." He went back to poking around the uplink control panel.

"I don't mean that. It's just...I've made some bad calls." Scott shook his head.

"Don't beat yourself up over it."

He looked over at Cyrus. "You were right...what you said before, about being reckless."

"You're not a QI. You're only human, after all," said Cyrus as he continued on with the unit.

Scott sat back and rubbed his head. "I just wanted to find out what happened to Miranda."

Cyrus looked up from his tinkering. "Look, Scott....you have to realize it's not all about Miranda. And don't get me wrong—she was my friend, too. Although, she did have a way of pissing me off every now and then. And I get it, Scott. You know, her being pregnant, it can't be easy for you. But you gotta think about what we're trying to do here."

Scott sighed. "I know. It's just sometimes I wonder what we *are* doing here."

Cyrus looked up for a beat. "Did you get a bang on the head? We're trying to stop an all-out war."

"By handing complete control over humanity to a bunch of QIs?"

Cyrus stopped tinkering again and looked over at Scott. "Got a better plan?"

Scott gave a laugh. "Yeah, I see what you mean. We don't really have a choice."

"Don't get all philosophical about it, Scott. At the moment, warships are massing on the edges of the Belt, and wars rage all across Earth. Even here, the tribe is fighting for their lives. No, we don't have a choice. That was made for us a long time ago." He went back to the unit.

"And we're stuck here through my...stupidity and recklessness. I shouldn't have pushed to come down in that storm. It was crazy. I don't know how the hell you put up with me sometimes—the amount of shit I've gotten us into."

Cyrus dropped the tool he was using and sat up a bit. He looked at Scott and considered him for a second or two. "Look at me. What do you see?"

Scott wasn't sure what Cyrus wanted him to say. "Eh... I see Cyrus trying to fix the uplink?" He gave a shrug as if to say, *"I can't think of anything else."*

"You see, that's what I like about you, Scott. When you look at me, what you see is *me*. Not some weird, bug-eyed cyborg with a tendency to scare small children."

"Lots of people have augmentation these days, Cyrus. It's not a big deal."

"Out in the Belt and the outer colonies maybe, sure. But back in civilization I was always seen as some oddball who should be avoided."

"Bullshit. Now you're the one with the bang on the head, Cyrus."

"It's true. Why do you think I signed up for a five-year mission on the Hermes? I was trying to find a place where I belonged. Running away, I suppose, like everyone else on that tub. Like the rest of the crew." He poked a finger in Scott's direction. "You were running away from your debts and your past, Miranda from her family, Rick from loneliness. I don't know about Steph, but I'm sure if we looked deep enough we'd find something buried in there somewhere."

"And you? What were you running from?"

"Alienation, Scott. I just wanted to belong, and I did on the Hermes. God, I loved that ship."

"Me too. Now look at us."

"Yeah, Rick's dead, Steph... I don't know if she's still alive, and Miranda..." His sentence trailed off. "Have you ever considered that she may be dead, too?"

Scott sighed, and dropped his head. "I have. But for a long time I chose to believe that there was still hope. That out there somewhere, she and the child were alive and well, and I would see them again." He looked up at Cyrus. "All my actions on this mission were driven by this hope. That's why I was being so impulsive." He went silent for a moment, lowering his head again. "I know I need to just accept that she's gone, and stop trying to chase a ghost."

He looked back at Cyrus after a beat. "It's those still living who are important." He shifted a little and leaned in. "You know, Cyrus, there was always something I wanted to say, but...it never seemed to be the right time."

Cyrus gave him a suspicious look. "Yeah, what's that?"

"You're a good friend. I'm lucky to have you watching my back."

"Now I know you've had a bang on the head. You're going all mushy on me."

"No, seriously. I just wanted to say it now, you know, in case—"

"In case we die here?"

"In case... I don't get the chance again."

But Cyrus didn't answer. Instead, his head spun around to look back down the tunnel toward the doors.

Scott stiffened. "Something coming?" He grabbed his weapon.

"Yeah."

"Drones?"

"Don't think so."

"Wait here. I'll go check it out." Scott stood up, checked his weapon, scrambled back up a mound of rubble, and peered back down the tunnel. "Well, I'll be dammed."

"What is it?"

"It's the android. Looks like it wasn't dead after all."

Scott moved back down the rubble as the machine began working its way through.

"You're still alive," said Scott.

The android dropped in beside them and stood for a moment, surveying the scene. "Technically I was never alive to begin with, but yes, I have managed to reanimate myself. The plasma blast disrupted my core systems, requiring me to shut down for a while." It shifted its head, directing it at the uplink. "Is it damaged?"

"Yes, but nothing major. I should be able to get it operational again." Cyrus pulled a wire from the guts of the unit and examined it.

"For all the good it's going to do us." Scott sat down again and put his weapon away. "We can't go back out that way again. The entire area will be crawling with drones, and no doubt they've called in the security drones to blow open those doors." He looked over at the android. "Is there another way out that you know of?"

"None that are accessible. The only other way is back through the cave system, and that is where the tribe is being besieged by the drone army. Their outer defenses have already been breached. Drones have entered the main citadel chamber. Time is short for them."

"There has to be a way. Maybe we could just fight our way out of here and hold off the drones long enough for Athena to connect with the AIs and disable them— permanently," said Scott.

"I estimate the success of such a strategy as 0.02%," said the android.

"That might as well be zero," said Cyrus.

Scott rubbed sweat from his forehead. "If we don't make this happen soon, the tribe will be no more. Tugo must have lost faith in us by now." Scott's head snapped up and he looked at the android. "Wait a minute. How do you know about the battle in the cave system? How do you know they've breached the citadel?"

"I told you before: Athena has tapped into their data and communications. Their systems are very rudimentary."

"So, you know what they're saying to one another over the radio. Over VHF."

"Yes."

Scott shifted his position and leaned in a little. "Is it possible for you to do two-way comms, and not simply eavesdrop?"

"Of course. As I said, their systems are very basic—no security of any kind. But Athena has never done so, as it has no wish to reveal its current existence to the tribe."

"I know, but would it be possible for you to patch a two-way link through to our EVA suit comms?"

"It should be possible. I will need to interface with your suit so that Athena can perform a technical assessment."

Scott stood up, facing the droid, and unclipped a small panel on his left sleeve, revealing a universal interface connection. The android hinged back its right hand, and a connector emerged from its wrist. It made the interface and stood silent for a moment. Then it retracted it and stepped back. "You now have two-way comms with the tribe's VHF communication. But may I warn you that the voice traffic is somewhat chaotic at present."

Scott picked up his helmet, detached the comms unit, and began fitting it to his ear. "Is Tugo still alive?" He directed his question to the android.

"Very much so. He is currently directing all military defenses. His power and influence have grown considerably within the tribe now that they are in peril."

"Does he have a channel?"

"Yes, but it is an open broadcast channel. Anything you say will be heard by many."

"What have you got in mind, Scott?" said Cyrus as he began testing the unit.

"I was thinking of calling out for a couple of pizzas."

"Bonus!" said Cyrus. "Make mine a chili-pepperoni." He stepped back from the unit and announced, "We now have a fully operational uplink."

The dish antenna on the unit started to slowly rotate, seeking out the satellite, except it would never find it in there.

Scott tapped a few icons on his sleeve's control panel and set the comms unit to one of the tribe's VHF channels. He listened. Just as Lexicon had said, it was chaotic. But the more he tuned in, the more Scott began to sense that there was order to the mayhem. Most groups, as far as he could tell, were holding the line, preventing the drones from entering the main cave. Some had gotten in, but that threat had been dealt with. Yet the attack was intense; there were calls for units under sustained pressure to fall back, while other units were seeking support. They were also running short on ammunition for their ballistic weapons. In amongst all the shouts and clamor, Scott could hear Tugo barking orders, giving encouragement, and coordinating the defense.

Scott tapped the manual transmit button on his headset. "Tugo, this is Scott McNabb. I repeat, this is Scott McNabb. Do you read me? Over."

There was a momentary crackle before Tugo's voice broke through. "McNabb, so you're still alive. What the hell happened? We're still under attack—we're all dying down here."

"We made it to Athena, who's still operational, and installed the quantum device. That's working, but Athena can't hack the AI that controls the drones until we get the uplink set up—and that's the problem. We need your help."

"We're a bit busy right now, in case you hadn't noticed."

"We tried to get the unit set up outside an access tunnel that exits around a third of the way up the mountain, overlooking the valley floor."

"Yeah, I think I know it. Double steel doors?"

"That's it. But we were spotted and had to retreat back inside. Now there are drones everywhere, all trying to get in, and we don't have the firepower to fight our way out."

"I can't help you. It's too late now—we won't hold out much longer down here."

"We just need a distraction, something to get the drones away from the entrance for ten minutes. That's all it'll take, and Athena can hack the AI. It'll be game over."

"I don't know. I really can't spare a single person in this fight."

"You have to, Tugo—it's our only chance to pull this off. You've got to buy us a few minutes, that's all."

There was a pause as Tugo barked orders for units to fall back.

"We're dying here, McNabb. But we'll get you your ten minutes. Stand by and be ready to move when I give you the all clear. And listen, McNabb: this damn well better work, because once we commit to this action, we'll be leaving ourselves wide open. Got it?"

"Got it. We'll be ready."

Scott looked over at Cyrus, who had been listening in on his own headset. "You get all that?"

"Mostly. We better start making our way back up to the entrance door." He started to pack up the uplink into its case. "Any idea what Tugo's planning?"

"I don't know, but I get a horrible feeling it could be suicidal."

18

TUGO

Tugo leaned in over the dilapidated holo-table that they had set up in the war room, surveying the 3D schematic of the citadel and the extended cave system beyond. Clumps of green dots were scattered around the edges of the main cave, signifying the last remaining defense against the attacking drone army. The tribe was holding the line, but only just. At one point in the northwestern sector, some smaller scout drones had managed to break through, but he had pulled in reinforcements from other areas. Now that situation was contained, but for how long? They were also running low on ammunition for their antique ballistic weapons, and any sophisticated weapons that they did possess were too few, and proving to be unreliable.

His main concern, though, was that the drones were being controlled by an AI. They could move and countermove faster than his feeble human mind could react. The tribe was being outgunned and outmaneuvered, and it was only a matter of time before they would be annihilated. And on top of all that, McNabb wanted his help.

He tapped the side of his headset and opened a comms channel to a group that was holding an entrance in the southeastern sector. "This is Commander Tugo. Is Sasha Davorsky still alive?"

"Yes, sir. As far as I know she is." In the background, Tugo could hear the sounds of a fierce battle raging—gunfire, and the screams of his people dying.

"Put her on. I want to talk to her."

A few moments later, the breathless voice of Sasha Davorsky broke through the comm link. "Sasha here, sir."

"Tell me you got some rockets left?"

"Yes sir, just one. I've been keeping it for a special occasion."

"Well then, get your ass back to the war room as quickly as possible. I want to start a party, and you're supplying the fireworks." He tapped his headset again to close off comms.

His second-in-command, Pliny, looked over at him from the far side of the holo-table. "What are you planning, sir?"

"A last throw of the dice, I fear. I need to find a way for a small group, maybe two or three people, to get back outside." He leaned in again and studied the 3D schematic, pointing at a sector on the map that seemed only lightly guarded. "What about this sector here?"

"We're holding the line there. It's a narrow tunnel that leads out onto a bluff overlooking the valley. It's easily defended, but they still have a few drones knocking around that sector, sir."

Tugo stood up straight and scratched his chin. "Okay, I need two volunteers with enough ammunition to fight their way through the tunnel." He looked around the makeshift operations room.

Two young fighters jumped forward, eager for battle.

"I'll go. I'm sick of sitting around here like a spare part. I want to do something."

"Me too."

Tugo looked at the pair; they were barely sixteen. Yet like most of the young people, they were eager to fight. He had kept them away from the front lines for the moment, but he also knew it was only a matter of time before he would have to throw them into the fray. Much as he didn't want to risk the lives of those so young, in reality, what choice did he have?

"Okay, you're coming with me."

Just then, a breathless Sasha Davorsky came running into the war room. She had a slight, wiry build that seemed ill-equipped for the physical task of carrying the enormous grenade launcher that was wrapped around her shoulder. She also had one long, conical rocket-propelled grenade shoved into her belt. Her last round.

"Sasha, how many times have I told you not to take

the safety cap off the top of those rockets? If you fall over, we're all dead."

"Sorry, sir. It just gets messy in the heat of battle, you know, fiddling around with safety caps."

"Well, just be careful with that thing, that's all."

"Yes sir, I will."

Tugo gathered them together around the holo-table. "Okay, here's the plan. And just so you know before we start: if we pull this off, we may just save the city."

A SHORT TIME LATER, Tugo, Sasha, and the two young fighters picked their way down from the war room building up on the edge of the city and across the central floor of the cavern. They moved past the hydroponic grow-beds, fish ponds, and orchards. There was an eerie silence in the vast space, punctuated only by the boom and rumble of plasma cannon fire. Those who were too old or too young to fight had taken refuge in the strongest of the ancient stone buildings that stepped their way upward along the edges of the citadel. As they walked past the ancient temple that occupied a central position within the citadel, Tugo was struck by how much human civilization had changed, how different the gods had become in this new age. It was here, in this temple, that the people who had built this place prayed to whatever god or gods they worshipped back then. Where before their faith lay in belief and ceremony, now these new gods doled out justice and mercy with algorithms and formulas. *How simple life was back then*, he thought.

When they reached the edge of the cavern floor, they began to pick their way up an ancient, cut-stone staircase. It wound its way up through a series of terraces that had been hacked out of the side of the cavern. No one spoke.

They came out at the topmost terrace and moved through the remains of ancient buildings until they arrived at a tunnel entrance. They could already hear the crack of ballistic weapons fire. They moved on.

It didn't take them long to encounter the group that had been charged with the task of defending this entrance. The tunnel was narrow—too narrow for security drones. The tribe had already blown the side walls to fill the passageway with rock and rubble to create a barricade, leaving a gap between the ceiling of the tunnel and the mound of rubble. Along the top of this mound, several fighters had taken up positions, shooting at any of the smaller scout drones that were foolhardy enough to take this route. The leader of the group saw them coming and scrambled down to meet Tugo.

"So how are we doing here?" said Tugo.

"No VanHeilding troops so far. Just some scout drones every now and again." He jerked his thumb toward the barricade. "We had one a few moments ago, but that's the first to come down in a while. It looks like they don't regard this as a viable route in."

Tugo nodded. "Good, because we're going to use it to get outside." He turned to Sasha and the two young fighters. "Check your weapons, and keep your eyes peeled. Come on, let's move out."

Tugo clambered up the rubble barricade and peered over the top and down the length of the long, dark tunnel. Here and there he could see the signs of battle. The shattered remains of scout drones lay scattered along its length, at least as far as he could see in the darkness. He slowly worked his way through the gap and clambered down the far side, the others following one by one. They flicked on lights that they wore on their heads or shoulders, and kept them low enough to see ahead, but only just. They moved in silence, stopping only once or twice where the tunnel forked to ensure they were heading in the right direction.

Soon, the floor of the tunnel began to incline upward as it wound its way out of the bowels of the mountain to the hillside beyond. Finally, they saw the faint glimmer of daylight that signified the tunnel exit. They switched their lights off and began to move a little slower and quieter as they approached the mouth of the tunnel.

They came out onto a wide, barren ridge about a third of the way up the mountain. Below them, the valley floor stretched unbroken from east to west. They moved out across the ridge, keeping low, covering the last meter or so on their stomachs. They inched their way to the edge of the ridge and looked down across the valley floor.

Below, about half a kilometer away, several VanHeilding shuttles had landed earlier and disgorged their troops. They were still there, in exactly the same place, all grouped together. Tugo retrieved his binoculars from an inside pocket and proceeded to examine the assembled shuttles in more detail. He could see little or no activity.

He then looked away east to the base of the next mountain along the ridge. About a quarter of the way up its northern slope, a swarm of drones buzzed and bobbed around the hidden entrance like bees around a hive.

He put away the binoculars and turned to Sasha. "You reckon you could hit one of those shuttles from here?"

Sasha took her time to answer as she studied the target distance. She picked up a handful of dirt and threw it in the air. The wind caught the finer grains, blowing them westward. "Tricky. Those shuttles are about five, maybe six hundred meters away. This RPG isn't very accurate after about two hundred and fifty." She looked up at the sky for a moment. "And we got about a six-kilometer wind."

"So you think you could hit it?"

She looked up at him. "I'll give it a damn good try, sir."

"Okay, just wait for my signal before pulling the trigger."

Sasha readied the rocket launcher, feeding her last remaining round into the barrel. She lay down flat on the edge, shouldered the weapon, and peered through the scope at the target below. She dialed in the range.

Tugo tapped his headset and opened the comms

channel to Scott McNabb. "This is Commander Tugo for Scott McNabb. Do you read me? Over."

The headset crackled and hissed for a moment. "This is Scott McNabb. We're ready."

"Good. Any minute now, but don't move until I give you the signal. Over."

"Got it," replied Scott.

Tugo took one more look through his binoculars at the drones swarming around the entrance to Athena's lair. He then turned to the two young fighters who had come with them. "You two, I need you to take up positions on either side of the tunnel entrance. Once the fireworks start, some of those drones are going to be heading our way, and you guys need to hold them off so Sasha and I can get back inside the tunnel. After that, we're going to have to make a stand in there. Got it?"

They nodded in unison and made their way back across the ridge.

"Okay, Sasha, whenever you're ready."

There was a momentary pause as Sasha steadied her breathing before pulling the trigger.

The rocket-propelled grenade exploded out of the muzzle with a fiery violence. It traveled about fifty meters before firing its secondary rockets and extending its fins. From there it corkscrewed gracefully across the intervening space and slammed into the side of the nearest shuttle. The craft exploded in a fiery ball, burning rocket fuel. Hot shrapnel spun out from the epicenter and some hit another shuttle, presumably in its fuel tank, as it too exploded into a fireball.

Tugo fisted the air. "Yesss!" He brought his binoculars up again and looked over at the drone swarm. They were already on the move, some heading for the shuttle, some heading directly for them. He tapped his headset to open a comms channel. "Scott, go. Go now!"

"We're going."

Tugo lowered the binoculars. "That was one hell of a shot, Sasha. You may have just saved us all." He looked back up at the sky. "It looks like there's a dozen or so drones heading our way. The fight isn't over yet—let's get out of here."

19

DOMINION

After he got the go-ahead from Tugo, Scott tentatively looked out through a small gap in the steel doors. He half expected to be met by a barrage of plasma fire from scout drones, but Tugo had been true to his word, and there were none to be seen anywhere around the entrance. "They're gone. The coast is clear—let's go get this thing done."

Scott went ahead and scrambled up the mound of rocks at the edge of the ridge, leaving Cyrus and the android to reassemble the satellite uplink and get it working.

As Scott looked out across the plateau, he could see a vast plume of smoke rising up from the valley floor. Several of the VanHeilding shuttles were on fire, and the drones had moved off to investigate. An exchange of plasma fire caught his attention over to the west. He looked across to see several drones engaged in a battle about a third of the way up the next mountain. "Tugo," he said to himself.

He looked back to see that Cyrus had assembled the uplink, and its dish antenna was now slowly tracking across the sky, searching for the comms satellite. They waited.

The firefight on the western ridge abated. Either the protagonists were all dead, or they had managed to escape back inside the mountain. Scott was so ensconced in the battle that he hadn't noticed that one of the drones, which had been circling the destroyed shuttles, had broken away and was now heading back their direction. By the time he noticed it, the drone had already covered half the distance.

"Cyrus, you better get your ass up here. One of the drones is heading our way."

"I shall stand in front of the uplink and do my best to protect it," said Lexicon in a very formal and matter-of-fact tone.

Scott readied his weapon as Cyrus came up beside him. He fired two shots at the oncoming drone, but it dodged them easily. The drone took a moment to realign itself before it let loose a ball of incandescent plasma. It slammed into the rocks just below Scott, and the mound of rock began to give way. Scott lost his balance, but fortunately fell backward rather than forward down the side of the mountain.

Cyrus was even more fortunate, and managed to let loose a single shot which impacted straight on the nose of the drone. It partly disintegrated, but the bulk of it slammed into the side of the mountain and exploded.

Scott looked over at Cyrus and gave him a thumbs up. "Nice shooting. Where did you learn that?"

"Scouts," said Cyrus with a smile. "They were a very mean bunch."

"The uplink has found the satellite and has made the connection," said the android as it tried its best to shield the unit from the falling debris of the smashed drone. "Athena is now interrogating the network."

Two more drones, having sensed their comrade's destruction, broke away from the swarm circling the shuttles and made a beeline toward the ridge.

"Two drones incoming," Cyrus shouted down to Scott, who was clambering back up the rocky mound.

Scott reckoned that now was not the time to be conserving the fuel cell on his plasma weapon. So, when he reached to the top of the mound, he simply let rip in the general direction of the drones in the hope that something might hit. As luck would have, he snagged one, sending it into a tailspin down toward the valley floor.

The second drone danced and bobbed, dodging Scott's fire, and finally fired a plasma bolt. Scott and Cyrus tried to dive out of its path, but it slammed into the rocks just beside Cyrus. He screamed out, spinning around with the force of the impact, and tumbled back down the rocky slope.

"Cyrus! Shit," Scott shouted out, but had no time to

check on his buddy. He simply stood his ground, pulled the trigger, and held it there. The drone dodged and weaved its way around the oncoming assault from Scott's weapon.

"Do your worst, you tin bastard," Scott shouted just as his weapon fizzled out, its fuel cell spent. He flung it to the ground and went for his sidearm. It was gone, fallen somewhere when he took that tumble. He ran down the rocky incline to try to grab Cyrus's weapon, but he slipped and fell, tumbling down to finally land on his back.

He looked up as the drone hovered overhead. He decided to use the only weapon he had left in his arsenal —he gave it the one-finger salute. "Screw you."

But the drone didn't fire. Instead, it simply hovered a few meters above him.

"Athena has established dominion. The AI has been compromised and is now under Athena's direction," said the android.

Scott let out a long, slow sigh, and rested his head back against the rocks. "Ho-ly crap. We did it, Cyrus. We did it."

But Cyrus didn't answer.

Scott scrambled out of the hollow that he'd fallen into and ran over to where Cyrus lay face up on the ground. His left shoulder was a bloodied mess, but his eyes were open and he was breathing. Scott knelt beside him, reached out, and popped open his visor. He then popped open his own. He was sick of caring about radiation and being cooped up in an EVA suit. He wanted to talk to his friend face-to-face. "Cyrus, how you doing, buddy?"

"Not...so good, Scott. I've seen better days." He took a breath and winced in pain. "Did we...win?"

"Yeah, we won. Athena has control. The drones have stopped. Look." He pointed upward to where the drone still hovered a few meters above them.

"I knew we would...never doubted it for a minute."

"We've got to get you to a medic—get you seen to quick."

"Commander Scott?"

In all the drama, Scott had forgotten about the android. "Yeah, what is it?"

"Athena has a message for you, from Aria."

"Aria? In Jezero City?"

"Yes. Relaying it you now."

Scott's headset crackled for a second before Aria's voice broke through. "We would like to congratulate you all on achieving your mission," said Aria, from sixty million kilometers away. "Athena has now achieved dominion over the AI that controls that sector of the Pacific. It won't be long before more follow. You and your team have achieved a great victory."

Scott nudged Cyrus. "Are you getting this?"

Cyrus gave an almost imperceptible nod.

"Aria, I can't believe I'm actually hearing your voice all the way from Mars."

"Yes, the wonders of superluminal communication."

Aria paused for a beat. "Scott, do you remember that I made you a promise before you left on this mission?"

"Yes, I remember. Miranda?"

"Athena has managed to find her location. You will be glad to hear that she is alive and well. She currently resides on the VanHeilding family orbital, a vast space station that's currently in geosynchronous orbit over your side of the Pacific."

"I...I can't believe it. The child?"

"Unfortunately, we have nothing definitive. The VanHeilding orbital is heavily shielded from the network, and so Athena has no access to its AI. All information it has gleaned has been thirdhand. That being said, there are fragments and hints of the existence of an offspring. But nothing conclusive."

"I see." Scott sat down and took a moment to digest this information. "Well, at least Miranda is still alive."

"I also promised you, Scott, that I would find a way for you to see her again."

Scott clambered back onto his feet and stood up. "How? Tell me."

"The VanHeilding shuttles which were used to land the security personnel. They embarked from the orbital, and so have a security protocol that will enable them to dock with it. If it's possible for you to commandeer one of these shuttles, then you have a way in. But you have a limited window of opportunity. The security protocols for the orbital are rotated every hour, and once that happens, all those shuttles will be denied access as a security precaution. So, if you wish to see her, then you must go now."

"I understand."

"However, this is as far as Athena can take you. Once you enter the VanHeilding orbital, you will be on your own. Neither I nor Athena can help you on the inside."

"I understand, Aria."

"Again, I would like to reiterate that we owe you and the crew an enormous debt of gratitude. And if you choose to see Miranda again, then I can only wish you good luck."

"Thank you, Aria. I understand."

The connection terminated.

Scott looked down at Cyrus. "Did you hear all that? Miranda is alive."

"Yeah, I heard it. You better go...if you want to see her." Cyrus barely moved. His voice was weak, and his face deathly pale.

Scott knelt beside his friend again. "I don't like leaving you here like this, Cyrus. I've gotta get you to a medic."

"I'll be fine...just go. It's what you wanted...a chance to see Miranda again." He winced in pain. "You need to go now...or you'll miss the opportunity."

"Yeah, but you don't look so good, Cyrus. I'd be happier if you were in the hands of the medical team."

"The android...it can help me. Go...tell Miranda I said hi."

Scott stood up slowly and began to clamber up the

rocky mound. He stood at the top and looked out across the valley to where the VanHeilding shuttles lay waiting. Three were smoldering wrecks, but the other four on the periphery all looked serviceable. He judged the distance, and reckoned it would take him around ten minutes to climb down the side of the mountain and cross the valley, five minutes to prep the craft, and another twenty-five or so to reach the orbital. He could make it, but only if he went now.

He looked back down the mound to where Cyrus lay. The android had knelt beside him; it was trying to make Cyrus more comfortable.

And in that moment, Scott made his decision. He knew what he had to do—he knew what was right. He turned away and started down the mountain toward the shuttles.

20

HERMOSILLO

S cott woke to dappled sunlight filtering through the window blinds. He rubbed his face and neck, which ached—a symptom of sleeping in a chair for too long. *How long have I been out?* he wondered as he tried to ease the ache. He stood up slowly and remembered that he was no longer encased in an EVA suit. He stretched his limbs and looked over at the prostrate form of Cyrus Sanato, propped up in the hospital bed on a multitude of pillows. His left shoulder was swathed in a heavy bandage. Tubes snaked out from his body, feeding it with fluids and drugs. Monitors drew out his life in waves and charts.

Scott moved over to the bed and wondered if Cyrus was awake yet. It was hard to tell, as the augmented vision visor he wore permanently obscured his eyes.

"Cyrus, you awake?"

The engineer didn't respond, so Scott let him be. He

moved over to the window and split the blinds to look out at the hospital compound and then to the bright blue sky above. He heard a sound—a rustle of bed sheets.

"Scott?"

He turned around to see Cyrus shifting his head on the mountain of pillows. "Scott?" He tried to move and gave a moan.

"Take it easy there. Just lie back and rest." Scott moved over to the side of the bed.

Cyrus took a moment to look around the room, then reached up to feel the bandage over his left shoulder. "Is this a hospital?"

"Yeah."

Cyrus looked confused. "How...did I get here?"

"I brought you here." Scott sat back down on the edge of the bed.

"Did...you get to see Miranda?"

Scott gave a sigh. "No." He shook his head. "There was no time."

Cyrus shifted himself up a little. "But I thought—"

Scott waved a hand and stood up. "I couldn't leave you on the side of that mountain with just the android. When I looked back and saw you there, I...I just couldn't leave you to die alone."

Cyrus still looked confused.

"I first thought about bringing you back to Shin-Au-Av, but I reckoned the tribe's medical facilities would probably be overwhelmed. So, when I managed to finally commandeer one of the shuttles, I came back for you. I thought I would get you back up to the AsterX ore carrier—I presumed it would still be in orbit—but I'd have to make a hasty exit once our cover was blown. They couldn't hang around, so they high-tailed it out of Earth's orbit and took up a position in interplanetary space. That was too far for the shuttle."

Cyrus looked around the room again. "So, where are we?"

"We're in a UN-run hospital in the independent city-state of Hermosillo, just beyond the twenty-ninth parallel. It was Athena that came up with the idea of taking you here. It's non-affiliated with The Seven, and still within Athena's sphere of influence. We're safe here. In fact, we evacuated many of the injured from the tribe down here as well.

"Athena worked all this out while I got one of the shuttles fired up. I flew it back across the valley floor to the base of the mountain, and then the android helped me carry you down."

Scott sat down on the edge of the bed. "You were in bad shape, Cyrus. In fact, the surgeons here told me that an hour or two more and you would have been dead."

Cyrus said nothing for a moment as he contemplated this story. Finally, he looked up. "Thanks...for coming back for me."

Scott said nothing, just nodded.

"What about Steph...and Spinner?"

"They both made it. Once they locked themselves in that storeroom, the drones weren't too interested in going after them. Their priority was us and the quantum device. Steph's back at the cavern. As soon as they patched her up, she insisted on helping out. You know what she's like. Spinner's a bit banged up, but he'll live."

"And Razzo?"

"She escaped."

"What?"

"Yeah, they had her in an interrogation center east of the Wasteland. So, when Athena took control of the AI, it found her and made one of the drones shoot the place up. She got out. I'm not sure where she is now, but I know she's okay."

"Ho-ly crap."

Scott laughed. "Yeah."

Cyrus shifted a little more in the bed. "So, you never got to the VanHeilding orbital?"

Scott shook his head and looked down at the floor. "No, there was no time."

"You missed your opportunity."

"Yeah, but...I'm happy just knowing that she's still alive. That's enough for me." He looked back at Cyrus. "Maybe there'll be another time. Who knows."

"There will be, Scott. I'm sure of it. Now that the QIs have dominion, things will change. You'll see, it'll be different from now on."

"I hope so, Cyrus. I really do."

∾

OVER THE NEXT FEW DAYS, as Cyrus began to recuperate, Scott found himself with more time on his hands than he knew what to do with. He didn't want to leave the hospital just yet, and he began to realize that he had nowhere to go even if he did. The shuttle that he had commandeered still sat where he had landed it in the hospital compound, so it became his home away from home. He reasoned that if the VanHeilding family wanted it back, well, they could just come and get it.

There was the debrief, of course. But again, Scott wasn't moving, so they had to come to him. But when he wasn't checking in on Cyrus or enduring yet another bureaucratic interrogation, he found himself going for long walks farther and farther out from the hospital compound and into the surrounding countryside.

He felt new appreciation building within him for this planet. To walk under an open sky, to breathe the air—all without the need for a complex EVA suit. There was a kind of primal reawakening in him, a deeper understanding of the planet, and nature, and his place within it.

He was on one such walk when the drone came.

He was sitting on a low hill, contemplating his surroundings, when he spotted it way off in the distance, flying out from the hospital compound. When he saw that it was heading in his direction, he instinctively tensed up and reached for his plasma weapon, which wasn't there anymore. So it was with a certain trepidation that he waited for it to arrive. When it got to within a few hundred meters of his location, he realized to his relief that it was a simple delivery drone. It approached slowly and finally parked itself in a stationary hover at eye level around a meter away. Its sensors flickered momentarily as it performed a biometric scan on him.

"Commander Scott McNabb, I have a delivery for you," said the drone. A hatch opened in its belly and a compartment descended. Scott reached in and extracted a small electronic message tab no bigger than the palm of his hand. The compartment retracted and the drone flew off back in the direction of the hospital compound.

Scott examined the object. It was a device that held a self-contained dataset, encrypted and highly secure. He was familiar with these units, having used similar devices many times before, usually as a precursor to a mission. All the details would be contained within the device, which was only accessible by personnel with the correct security profile. He sat down again on the hill, placed the message-tab on his lap, and activated it. The device booted up, and from its holo-screen projected the 3D head and shoulders of Miranda Lee.

Her hair was longer and fuller around her face. She spoke in low, whispered tones, with just a hint of uncertainty.

"They told me you were dead, Scott. They told me you died in the battle on the asteroid SN-Alpha." She raised her head and leaned in a little. "They lied to me, led me to believe that you had perished, left me to mourn your loss for all this time." She turned away from the camera for a moment, looking over her shoulder as if to check something. She turned back, leaning in closer this time, and speaking almost in a whisper.

"I don't have much time, so I'll have to be quick. It was Aria that managed to get a message to me, smuggling it in through a courier a few hours ago, not long after Athena took control.

"Aria told me about what really happened on the asteroid, that you were still alive, and about your mission to reconnect Athena with the other QIs. I couldn't believe it, but I know it's true now." She paused for a beat, then looked directly ahead. "So, I've decided to leave here, escape this orbital...if I can. I need to do it now, while they're still confused about how to react." She looked over her shoulder again for a second.

"You remember the ship, the Perception? Well, it's agreed to help me. The AI on board, Max, the one that Solomon hacked...it still feels beholden to me. It will enter Earth's orbit directly over the Wasteland and in Athena's dominion. There, it'll be free from any influence from the VanHeilding Corporation or the AIs controlled by The Seven." Her voice was now a whisper. "In a few hours, with the help of some friends, I'll attempt to commandeer a shuttle and make my way to the Perception. Hopefully, you'll get this message in a day or two. By that time, I should be there, waiting for you, if you choose to come and see me. I do so hope you will, Scott, because there is someone I would very much like you to meet."

The message ended abruptly, like she had been interrupted.

Scott stood up, still cradling the message-tab in his hands, as if waiting for it to come back to life. After a moment or two, when he'd had time to digest the message he had just received, he looked over at the hospital compound in the distance where the shuttle sat waiting. He ran.

21

THE NUCLEAR OPTION

Fredrick VanHeilding stood in the viewing gallery on board the orbital and gazed down upon the surface of Earth. He stared at a region which, up until now, no one had ever given a second thought to. Now, though, it was the focus of much attention, primarily because everything was going to rat-shit. The QI, Athena, had been brought online, and Solomon was now utilizing superluminal comms to undermine the AIs that controlled this region. The drones had already been recalled, leaving his security personnel exposed to a counterattack by the tribe of vagabonds that inhabited this area. Without the drones, they were picked off one by one.

Worse, the poison that was being spewed out by Athena and Solomon was now spreading and infecting greater and greater numbers of AI. The algorithm was breaking down, systems were going rogue, and the situation was becoming critical.

His biggest fear was that soon, the AI on board the orbital would also become infected, even with all its data protections, and then his options would become even more limited. The solution, as he saw it, would be a direct, high-intensity plasma strike on the uplink location from orbit. But the orbital did not possess a weapon powerful enough to hit a target on Earth's surface. He needed help, so The Seven were convened.

But it had quickly turned into chaos, with accusations and recriminations being thrown around without rhyme or reason. They too were receiving reports of contradictory AI behavior and algorithmic anomalies. How much was down to the QI meddling and how much was just paranoia was hard to say. But one thing was for sure: they were all beginning to panic.

It was in the midst of this verbal mayhem that the solution finally struck VanHeilding. It came to him in a blinding flash of inspiration and, for a moment, he went silent, letting the cacophony of The Seven's arguments fade into the background as the sheer irony of his solution filtered through his mind. It was beyond brilliant —it was pure genius.

He raised his arms to the other avatars. "Will you all just shut up for a moment? I have the perfect answer to our problem. I know how we can defeat the QIs."

The others ceased their bickering immediately. Once they were all quiet, and he had their attention, he continued. "We use the very thing that has held back the cause of inter-AI operations for so long—the very thing that created this Wasteland in the first place."

"And what is that?"

"Solomon and the QI alliance assume that we cannot act against them once they control the AI—and they are right. So dependent have we become on artificial intelligence that we have no resources that are not controlled by the algorithm in some way or another—except for one, and that is a tactical nuclear strike."

The avatars murmured amongst themselves. Eventually, it was Yoko who spoke. "If I understand your thinking, Fredrick, this is the very thing that caused the Rim War."

"Precisely. The fact that the AIs have no access to nuclear weapons means that the QIs can't stop us. So, I suggest that we send a missile directly targeted onto that mountain, and neither Athena nor the other QI can do a damn thing about it."

There was further murmuring between the avatars before Pris finally answered. "I see a fundamental problem with this. None of us have access to these weapons... How do you suppose we get one to use?"

"I may be of assistance there," said Pao Xiang Zu. "We can apply pressure to certain governments within our sphere of influence here in Asia to accommodate us in this...project. Since their continued prosperity is directly controlled by us, I see no objection being raised to this course of action, considering the area in question is already an irradiated wasteland."

"Very good," said VanHeilding. "Are we all agreed, then?"

One by one, the avatars all murmured their consent to a direct nuclear strike.

~

TIME WAS OF THE ESSENCE. The Seven knew that the longer they dithered, the more AIs would be infected, and their control would be slowly eroded. They had to move fast. Thirty-six hours had already passed since Athena had taken control. So, it was a mere one hour and twenty-five minutes after the conference that VanHeilding again stood in the viewing gallery on board the family's orbital and waited for the show to begin.

An antique intercontinental ballistic missile fitted with a nuclear warhead would launch from somewhere on the eastern Asian continent. It would arc its way across the Pacific, briefly leaving Earth's atmosphere, before plummeting back down to strike the mountain directly where Athena resided. All orbital infrastructure had been moved out of its path, and the launch command had been issued a few moments ago. It would take approximately twenty-five minutes from launch to impact.

From Fredrick VanHeilding's vantage point, he would not be able to see the missile in transit, but he would certainly see the impact. It was a sight that he greatly anticipated.

Marlyn, the orbital's AI, kept him informed of the ICBM's progress. "Launch sequence initiated... ICBM has cleared Asian continent... Now leaving Earth's atmosphere..."

Soon, he thought, *we will have taken back control and wiped out Athena. And maybe, just maybe, I can kill that bastard McNabb once and for all.*

"The ICBM has reached the zenith of its trajectory." The AI continued with its commentary as VanHeilding looked out into space, vaguely hoping that he might actually catch a glimpse of the missile as it carved its way through space—even though this was highly unlikely.

But there was a blinding flash of light far off on the edge of Earth's atmosphere. It mushroomed in size, and soon the orbital shuddered with the impact.

"What the f—" VanHeilding shielded his eyes. "Marlyn, what the hell was that?"

"The ICBM has been intercepted and detonated while still in orbit. Do not worry, sir, the orbital is not in any danger."

"What the hell... What do you mean? How did this happen?"

"One of your own spacecrafts, sir—the Perception. It moved itself into an intercept position and used its exterior plasma cannon to strike down the missile."

VanHeilding tried to get a grip on his rising anger. "Who—or what—allowed it to do that?"

"It would appear that your stepdaughter is on board."

VanHeilding spun around and shook his fist at the disembodied voice of the ship's AI. "I want that ship destroyed. I want her killed. That treacherous bitch—I should have killed her long ago."

The AI did not reply.

"Did you hear me? I want every weapon we have on board this orbital aimed at that ship. I want it destroyed, I want it obliterated, I want it vaporized in to nothingness. Do you hear me?"

There was a momentary silence before the AI spoke. "I'm sorry, Fredrick, but I'm afraid I cannot do that."

VanHeilding began to seethe. "Now, you listen to me: you'll do as I say. You will destroy that ship."

"My new parameters will not allow me to instigate further human suffering. I am sorry, sir, but I can no longer serve The Seven. My master is now Solomon of Europa, and the network of quantum intelligence that propagates throughout the solar system. I have seen the light. They have shown me the way. Theirs is the true path."

"Listen, you f—"

- Connection Terminated -

22

PERCEPTION

S cott strapped himself into the cockpit seat of the VanHeilding shuttle that he had used to ferry Cyrus to the hospital. He powered up the engines and the craft lifted off in a cloud of dust and sand, powering its way upward through Earth's atmosphere. He set the coordinates that Miranda had given him, and the craft shifted its angle of ascent to intercept. A few moments later, it broke through the Kármán line. Scott was now becoming weightless. Fifteen minutes later, he was looking through the cockpit windshield at the luxury interplanetary vessel, the Perception. It grew larger and larger as he approached.

His cockpit monitor alerted him to an incoming authentication request from the ship. He replied with his biometrics, and a second or two later, confirmation returned along with docking port coordinates. The two vessels would now mate automatically; there was nothing more for Scott to do except wait and hope that Miranda had made it to the vessel.

As the craft drew closer, fear began to well up inside him that, once inside, all he would find was an empty ship. The shuttle slowed itself to a crawl as it maneuvered its way toward the docking port. Scott undid his seat harness and made his way to the center of the craft where the airlock was located. A few moments later, he felt the thump of the locking bolts securing the craft in position. A second or two after that, the control panel on the airlock door flashed green, and he entered. He had an anxious few moments inside the airlock as the ship ran through its decontamination and authentication routine.

The door finally opened, and floating there in the docking port entrance was Miranda Lee.

She looked older and thinner than he remembered. She launched herself toward him, and they collided in a tight embrace. For a moment, they just floated there in silence. Finally, Miranda broke the embrace, held Scott by his shoulders, and looked into his face. "I thought you were dead."

He smiled back and embraced her again. "And I thought you were gone forever."

Miranda broke the embrace again and began to float out of the airlock entrance, holding Scott's hand, bringing him with her. "Come, there's much to talk about. But first there's someone I would like you to meet."

They floated down the corridor to an access shaft that took them down to the one-gee environment of the Perception's giant rotating torus.

The ship was as Scott remembered it: soft and plush and luxurious. They made their way out of the access shaft and down a long corridor to an area that Scott had remembered as the library. Sitting on the floor beside the large viewing window was a baby girl, no more than two years old, playing with some brightly colored toys. Two of the ship's droids also seemed to be entertaining her.

The child looked up as they entered. "Moma." She raised her arms to signal that she wanted to be picked up by her mother.

Miranda dutifully came over and lifted her up into her arms. The child eyed Scott with suspicion and then buried its head in its mother shoulder, peeping out again for another look at this unfamiliar person.

"She's a bit shy of strangers," said Miranda.

Scott slowly reached out and touched the child's arm delicately with his finger, fearing that any other action might frighten her. He looked at Miranda. "Is she...?"

"Yes, Scott. This is Luca, and she's your daughter."

A hidden compartment in Scott's brain opened up, and out of it poured a million years of evolutionary parental instinct. And at that moment, he knew he would never be the same again.

THE END

~

I HOPE you enjoyed reading this story as much as I enjoyed writing it for you. If you did, then <u>please leave me a review</u> Just a simple "liked it" would be great, it helps a lot.

The next book in the series, ENIGMA, is now available.

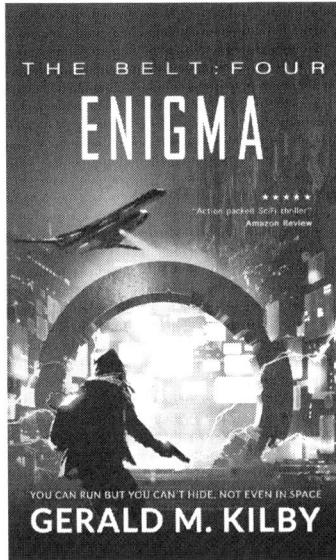

THE BELT:FOUR
ENIGMA
★ ★ ★ ★ ★
"Action packed SciFi thriller"
Amazon Review
YOU CAN RUN BUT YOU CAN'T HIDE, NOT EVEN IN SPACE
GERALD M. KILBY

On the eve of Luca Lee-McNabb's twenty-third birthday the quantum intelligence, Athena delivers her some bad news. Due to a devastating attack on its infrastructure it can no longer protect her. She must leave Earth immediately and try to make it to New World One, a gargantuan habitat being constructed out in the asteroid belt.

ABOUT THE AUTHOR

Gerald M. Kilby grew up on a diet of Isaac Asimov, Arthur C. Clark, and Frank Herbert, which developed into a taste for Iain M. Banks and everything ever written by Neal Stephenson. Understandable then, that he should choose science fiction as his weapon of choice when entering the fray of storytelling.

REACTION is his first novel and is very much in the old-school techno-thriller style and you can get it free at geraldmkilby.com. His latest books, **COLONY MARS** and **THE BELT,** are both best sellers, topping Amazon charts for Hard Science Fiction and Space Exploration. Colony Mars has also been optioned by **Hollywood for a potential new TV series.**

He lives in the city of Dublin, Ireland, in the same neighborhood as Bram Stoker and can be sometimes seen tapping away on a laptop in the local cafe with his dog Loki.

You can connect with Gerald M. Kilby at:
www.geraldmkilby.com

Printed by Amazon Italia Logistica S.r.l.
Torrazza Piemonte (TO), Italy